RANGER'S APPRENTICE

THE ROYAL RANGER BOOK 5

ESCAPE FROM FALAISE

RANGER'S APPRENTICE

THE ROYAL RANGER BOOK 5

ESCAPE FROM FALAISE

JOHN FLANAGAN

PHILOMEL BOOKS

PHILOMEL BOOKS
An imprint of Penguin Random House LLC, New York

Published in Australia by Penguin Random House Australia in 2021
Published in the United States of America by Philomel Books,
an imprint of Penguin Random House LLC, 2021

Visit us online at penguinrandomhouse.com.

Library of Congress Cataloging-in-Publication Data is available.

Manufactured in Canada

ISBN 9780593113486

FRI

1 3 5 7 9 10 8 6 4 2

US edition edited by Kelsey Murphy
US edition designed by Ellice M. Lee
Text set in Adobe Jenson Pro

RANGER'S APPRENTICE

THE ROYAL RANGER BOOK 5

ESCAPE FROM FALAISE

1

"TIE THEM UP," BARON LASSIGNY ORDERED. "THEY'RE UNDER arrest."

Maddie and Will stood silently while two of Lassigny's men moved forward, plucked the Rangers' saxe knives from their scabbards and tossed them to one side. Then they quickly bound Will's and Maddie's hands in front of them. Maddie tried to tense her wrists so that the bonds would loosen slightly when she relaxed them. But the soldier was awake to that trick. He slapped her wrists with the back of his hand.

"That's enough of that," he ordered roughly.

She shrugged and released her muscles, and he strained the cord tight, preventing any possible movement. Before long, she felt her hands growing numb from the restricted blood flow.

Lassigny gestured to Prince Giles, who was looking slightly dazed and confused by the rapid sequence of events. "Take him back to his room," he ordered.

A third man seized Giles's forearm and led him away. The prince went without protest. Lassigny turned his attention back to Will and Maddie. "These two go to the dungeon," he said.

Will and Maddie exchanged a glance. Will shrugged. There

was nothing they could do to resist. They were bound and unarmed. The men who had tied their hands now drew their daggers and stepped behind the two Rangers. Lassigny, seeing they were offering no resistance, sheathed his sword and pointed toward the stairs.

"Get moving," he ordered.

Will hesitated for a second and felt the sharp point of a dagger pressing into his back. He took the hint and began to move toward the staircase, Maddie beside him and the two men-at-arms following close behind. Lassigny and the other three soldiers followed a few meters back.

They went down the stairs, passing the guardroom level with the castle's battlements, where several yawning guards peered curiously at the little procession. Reaching ground level, they exited into the bailey. The prisoners hesitated, not sure which way they were meant to be heading. Another prod with the dagger directed them to the keep.

"You could have just told me," Will protested mildly. The dagger was sharp and the prodding was none too gentle.

"Shut up," he was told. He shrugged and moved toward the heavy door that led into the keep. This time, mindful of the need to avoid another jab with the dagger, he seized the iron ring of the door handle with his bound hands and opened the door, leading the way inside.

"Which way now?" he asked as they entered the keep.

"Down," the guard told him, gesturing toward the stairs in the center of the vast hall. Will headed toward them, but a word from Lassigny stopped him as he reached the head of the stairs.

"Put them in the eastern cells," the Baron said. The guard acknowledged the order with a grunt, and Lassigny continued, speaking to Will and Maddie for the first time since they had started down from the tower.

"We'll talk in a few days," he said.

"Do we have anything to talk about?" Will asked.

Lassigny smiled—a smile totally devoid of humor. "Oh, I think we do," he said icily. "We'll see how a few days in the cells will loosen your tongue. Perhaps you can sing for me again."

He turned away and mounted the stairs that led to the higher levels of the keep, heading for his quarters. Will felt another jab in his back.

"All right. All right," he said, and started down the stairs. His ever-present shadow went after him, with Maddie and her guard following. The other three men-at-arms continued with them, their boots clomping on the wooden stairs.

One level down, the stairs changed to rough stone and the air was noticeably cooler and damper. The stone stairs wound down for two more levels, then the two captives were guided to the right.

The walls down here were rough-hewn stone. Burning torches in wall sconces provided a dim light as they moved along a narrow, low-ceilinged passageway to where an iron gate was set in the wall.

"Stop here," Will's guide told him. Apparently, the dagger was only used for commands that involved going, not stopping. Then he called out, his voice echoing along the stone-lined passageway.

"Marius! Where are you?"

They heard a muttered exclamation from the darkness farther along the passage, then a door creaked open on complaining hinges, allowing yellow lamplight to flood into the passage. A heavily built figure, stooping under the low headroom, shuffled out of the doorway and headed toward them.

"Coming! Coming!" he called, his voice rough and throaty. He shambled toward them, his gait a curious shuffling hop, and stopped to survey them. The light from the nearest torch showed a heavy-browed face, with shaggy eyebrows and a tangled, matted beard. The nose had been flattened at some stage, presumably by a heavy blow, and never reset properly, so that it spread across his face, angled slightly to one side. Beneath the brows, the eyes were black and pitiless.

He smiled as he saw them, revealing that most of his teeth were missing.

"Ah, our new guests have arrived, I see," he said. He laughed. It wasn't a pleasant sound, and it caused the bunch of large keys hanging from his broad leather belt to jangle loudly.

The guard behind Will stirred slightly. Will sensed that he wasn't altogether comfortable here, in the presence of the jailer.

"Just open up and let them in," he said shortly.

"All in good time, Ramon," the jailer replied in that same throaty whisper.

He took a large iron key from the bunch hanging at his waist and opened the gate to allow them into the corridor beyond. "Let's take a look at who we've got here," he said.

He stepped closer to Will, peering into his face. Close up, his body odor and sour breath were all too evident.

"Why, if it isn't our songbird," he mused. Then he moved on to study Maddie's features as well. "And his lovely daughter." Maddie stood her ground as he crouched to place his ruined face close to hers. "Welcome to my lovely home," he told her, and laughed aloud again.

In spite of herself, Maddie flinched.

"Open the cell," Ramon insisted. The corridor was lined with cells on either side, each enclosed by another barred gate.

The jailer stepped back away from Maddie. He inserted the same key in the lock of one of the gates. It squealed as he heaved it open. Then he gave a clumsy parody of a bow as he ushered the two prisoners into the cell.

"Please, my dear guests, make yourself comfortable."

"Get inside," Ramon told them curtly. It was plain that he was eager to be out of this place and away from the jailer.

Will and Maddie needed no further urging. They stepped inside and Marius slammed the squealing gate shut behind them, rattling the key in its lock and testing that it was secure with several hearty tugs at the bars.

"Hands," Ramon told them, gesturing at a horizontal gap in the bars. Realizing what he meant, Will put his bound hands out through the gap and allowed Ramon to cut his bonds with the dagger. Maddie hurried to do the same, sighing with relief as the rough cord fell away from her wrists and blood started to flow through her hands again.

"Be careful with this one," Ramon whispered, nodding his head toward the huge, unkempt jailer. "He'll kill you as soon as look at you."

"Thanks for the warning," Maddie said in a lowered voice, rubbing her wrists together and wincing at the pain of returning circulation.

Ramon glanced back at the hulking jailer behind him. "Take care of them," he warned Marius. "The Baron wants to talk to them in a couple of days. And he wants them able to answer."

Marius made a pretense of bowing again, sweeping his hand down toward the stone floor.

"Oh, I will, I will," he said. "I'll have servants bring them hot food and drink and warm, soft bedding." He spoke with mock concern, then let out a bellow of laughter and turned away, heading back toward his own lair. "Hot food and warm bedding," he repeated, then laughed again.

But there was no food of any kind, and the bedding was a thin layer of filthy straw spread over the damp stone floor. The cell itself was lit by the torchlight from the passageway outside. Will and Maddie looked around, surveying their surroundings. In the dim light, there was little detail they could make out.

"Welcome to our new home," Will said.

Maddie frowned. "It's not exactly a palace, is it?"

Her mentor shrugged. "At least it's warm and dry," he told her, but she snorted disdainfully.

"It's not warm and it's certainly not dry," she said.

The room was cold, with that penetrating, bone-chilling cold that comes from being several floors underground and never having seen the light or warmth of the sun. The cold seemed to leech out of the stone walls. And the dim light showed several glistening black puddles of water on the floor.

Will sighed. "Well, you can't have everything."

2

THEY SCRAPED THE STRAW TOGETHER TO FORM A THIN COVER over the stone floor and, wrapped in their cloaks, rested their backs against the wall. The damp cold of the place quickly seeped through the cloaks. In the dim light, they could see little of their surroundings.

After an hour or so, they heard Marius shuffling along the passageway as he renewed the torches that provided light. Then the door of what they assumed was Marius's room banged shut and they heard no more of him. A little later, Maddie managed to doze off and slept fitfully. They passed the rest of the night in cold discomfort.

Surprisingly, when they awoke, they could see daylight. One side of the cell formed an air shaft about two meters by one that reached to the surface. Standing in the open space, they could look up and see an iron grating above them. Occasionally, a shadow would pass across it as someone walked by.

"It must open onto the courtyard," Will said.

The shaft allowed light and air to reach the dungeon, albeit in limited quantities. Unfortunately, it also allowed the rain in, which accounted for the several large puddles they could now see more clearly. As the light grew stronger, they took advantage of it to explore their surroundings. There was little enough to see. It was a large room, perhaps ten by seven meters, with a low-hanging ceiling that matched that of the passageway outside. The floor was solid rock and the walls were roughly worked stone fitted together without any sign of mortar. In one corner was a roughly screened-off section that served as a privy. Will glanced inside and sniffed carefully.

"Use only in dire need," he muttered as he emerged.

Aside from that, the room was devoid of any furnishing. Several sets of manacles hung on rusty chains from one wall.

"Don't like the look of those," Maddie remarked.

Will nodded. "Best stay on the right side of friend Marius," he replied.

Judging by the light in the shaft, they estimated that it must be about eight in the morning when they heard the jailer approaching. He peered in through the bars at them and chuckled throatily.

"I see my songbirds are awake," he said. "And just in time for breakfast: warm rolls and hot coffee."

He shoved a wooden tray through the gap in the door where Ramon had cut their bonds the night before, balancing it on the broad iron plate that formed the bottom of the gap. Will moved forward to take the tray but, as he did so, Marius snatched it back out of his reach.

"Say thank you," Marius demanded, giggling to himself.

"Thank you," Will said.

Marius kept the tray just out of his reach. "Thank you, kind Marius," he prompted.

"Thank you, kind Marius," Will said.

But still the tray was kept hovering just beyond his reach. "Thank you, kind, generous Marius."

"Th—" Will began, but the jailer forestalled him.

"Thank you, good, kind, generous Marius for our delicious breakfast."

With a great effort, Will stopped himself from showing his growing irritation with this childish farce. There was no point, he realized, in antagonizing this monstrous creature.

"Thank you, good, kind, generous Marius for our delicious breakfast."

Again, Marius let out a high-pitched giggle—an unpleasantly incongruous sound coming from such an enormous figure. But this time he returned the tray to where Will could reach it and bring it inside the cell.

"Why, no trouble at all," he said and turned away, shuffling off to his room down the passageway and giggling to himself. Will shook his head and let out a long, pent-up breath.

"Is it really rolls and coffee?" Maddie asked, rising on tiptoe to peer over his shoulder at the tray.

"Are you kidding?" Will said heavily. The tray held two pewter cups, a battered pewter jug of cold water and two stale bread rolls, one slightly tinged with mold.

"Oh," said Maddie. "I thought it sounded too good to be true."

"You're very gullible," Will told her. He took the moldy bread roll. "I'll have this one."

Maddie nodded her thanks. "I'm grateful."

They ate and drank quickly. While the food was less than appetizing, they were both hungry—and thirsty. Will poured the water, which seemed clean enough, into the cups, leaving half of it in the jug.

"Don't know when we'll get more," he said.

He placed the tray back on the iron shelf in the door and returned to his position by the wall, sliding down to sit on the floor and leaning back against the rough stone.

"What now?" Maddie asked. She was sitting a few meters along from him, in the same position. There was little other choice. At least the floor was drier here, as it was slightly higher against the wall and the water on the floor tended to pool in the lower sections.

"I guess we sit and twiddle our thumbs until Lassigny deigns to talk with us," Will said.

"Twiddle," Maddie said, considering the word with her head cocked to one side. "Exactly how does one twiddle, I wonder? And why doesn't one twaddle?"

"Twiddling is a well-established practice," Will told her. "And twaddle is what you're talking now."

Maddie sighed deeply. Aside from the cold, the discomfort and the unpalatable food, one of the unpleasant aspects of being cooped up like this was sheer boredom. There was a complete lack of anything to do, anything to see or listen to. And for an energetic young person like her, the lack of activity and stimulus was well-nigh unbearable.

True, she had been trained to spend long periods of time lying in wait and remaining immobile and silent. But at such times, she was *in wait*. She was remaining still in the expectation of something happening, of imminent action.

Here, the only likely event would be the arrival of their jailer with another unappetizing meal. Hardly something to look forward to.

"I wonder what Lassigny has in mind?" she mused. "How long

do you think he'll leave us here? He did say he planned on talking to us, didn't he? So when do you think he's going to do that?"

"Bored?" Will asked her, a note of sympathy in his voice.

"Absolutely, and it's not even midmorning yet," she replied.

He nodded several times. "Maybe you could try doing what I do when I'm bored," he suggested.

She turned to look at him. "What's that?"

"I sit quietly and don't bother the people around me."

Rebuked, she leaned back against the wall, shifting several times to find a relatively more comfortable spot. No matter how much she wriggled, there always seemed to be a rough outcrop that dug into her. She sighed once more but Will ignored her.

After a few minutes, she spoke again.

"Maybe we could trick him into letting us escape," she suggested.

Will eyed her bleakly. "By *him* I assume you mean that unpleasant man-mountain down the passageway?" She nodded. "How would we do that, do you think?"

"Well, I could pretend to be sick. I could moan and scream in pain and you could call him and get him to come in and see if I was all right."

"And then?"

"And then you could overpower him and we could get out of here."

"Two problems," Will said. "One, I doubt that Marius would give a moldy fig if you moaned and screamed all day. He'd probably enjoy it, in fact."

He paused while she took that in.

Then she asked: "What's the other problem? You said there were two."

"How exactly would I overpower him? Have you seen the size of him? He's a monster. He's three times as big as I am."

Maddie paused. She hadn't thought through that small detail. "Well, I'd help you, of course."

Will shook his head wearily. "Even with two of us combined, he's still twice as big."

"We could knock him out with something," Maddie suggested.

Will waved a hand around the bare cell. "With what? A handful of straw?"

Maddie surveyed the room. "There's the water jug?" she said hopefully.

"Yes, there is," Will replied. "And with that and a length of lead pipe, I might be able to overpower him."

Another silence ensued. Then: "I still have my throwing knife," Maddie said.

Will nodded. "Me too."

Surprisingly, Lassigny's men had neglected to search them when they were captured, simply taking their saxes and throwing them to one side. Will's smaller throwing knife was still strapped to his left forearm and Maddie's was concealed in a sheath below her collar. "But even so," he continued, "are you prepared to kill him in cold blood?"

She shifted uncomfortably. "Not really."

Silence fell once more. This time, she was surprised when, after several minutes, Will broke it.

"How did he know?"

She looked at him, frowning. "How did who know?"

"Lassigny. How did he know we were planning to rescue Giles? He was obviously expecting it. Even Marius wasn't surprised when we were brought in. He'd been told to expect prisoners. So how did Lassigny know?"

"Maybe he's just naturally suspicious?" Maddie ventured, but Will shook his head.

"There was nothing to connect us to Prince Giles," he said. "That was the whole point of Philippe asking for outsiders to do the job." He paused for several seconds. "Someone must have betrayed us."

"Betrayed us? Who could have done that? Who *would* have?"

Will turned slowly and met her gaze with his own.

"That's the big question, isn't it?"

3

THERE WAS A VIOLENT THUNDERSTORM THAT NIGHT.

The lightning flared down the light well, leaving a vivid afterimage of the shape of the opening that took seconds to fade. The thunder was horrific, rolling and booming in the night sky, setting the walls and floor of the cell vibrating, even so far under the ground.

But even more disconcerting than the effects of the storm were the sounds from their jailer's room, farther along the passageway. Marius was obviously terrified by the storm. He wept and howled in fear with each shattering clap of thunder, each flaring burst of lightning as it reflected up the dim passageway.

Eventually, the storm moved on in the small hours of the morning, and Marius's cries were reduced to a quiet sobbing, which still carried plainly to the two prisoners.

"Are you awake?" Will asked, as the thunder rolled in the distance.

"Who could sleep through that?" Maddie pulled her cloak tighter around her neck. In addition to the thunder and lightning, rain had poured down the air shaft, in huge drops that shattered on the stone floor and rebounded around the room. Maddie and Will had crept farther and farther away from the opening, watching the tide of rainwater slowly lapping toward them.

She was reminded of the storm they had gone through en route to Lassigny's castle, and she contrasted the warmth and security she had felt huddled under her blankets in the cart, Bumper's soft nose only a few inches away through the canvas, with the dank, cold conditions here in the dungeon. Involuntarily, she shivered.

When Marius brought their meal just after daybreak, he was haggard and his eyes were red-rimmed and wild. He was obviously still affected by his disturbed night. Will stepped toward the barred gate, taking the tray and moving quickly back out of the jailer's reach to where Maddie was waiting. Marius eyed them balefully as they sat on the floor, leaning forward over the food and water. Then, with a dismissive grunt, he turned away and shambled back to his lair.

But any potential problem with Marius was solved in the midmorning, when Ramon and three armed men arrived at the dungeon, shouting for him to open the gate. The hulking jailer shuffled down the passageway from his room, taking the huge iron key from his belt ring once more. Ramon sneered at him, noting the still-red eyes and furtive expression.

"Enjoy the storm then?" he asked sarcastically.

Marius, hunched over the lock, peered up at him.

Ramon suddenly waved both his hands apart and stepped forward. "Boom!" he shouted, and laughed as Marius cringed away from him.

"I wouldn't get him angry," Will cautioned.

But Ramon snorted. "There are four of us and he's unarmed. And he knows it," he said. "Frankly, I'd like him to try something against us."

He gestured to Marius to open the cell door and the jailer complied, scowling. Clearly there was little love lost between the guard and the big jailer.

Will shook his head. "One day you may not have him outnumbered," he said. But Ramon merely snorted once more, then gestured for the two Rangers to move out of the cell.

"Where are we going?" Will asked, but Ramon wasn't forthcoming.

"You'll find out," he said brusquely. "Give us your hands."

The other three soldiers had drawn their daggers as the gate was unlocked. They were keeping a watchful eye on the two prisoners, ready for any sign of rebellion.

"Do as he says," Will told Maddie. He held out his hands, crossed at the wrists, and Ramon quickly and expertly whipped a short length of cord around them, tying him securely. He did the same for Maddie as she held out her hands. This time, he let out a short burst of laughter as he noticed she didn't try to hold her wrists tensed.

"Learned your lesson, have you?" He grabbed her by the upper arm and turned her roughly toward the exit. "Let's go."

Two of the soldiers led the way. The other marched beside Ramon, a few paces behind Will and Maddie. They both had their daggers drawn and kept them only a few inches away from the prisoners. Thankfully, this time they didn't resort to poking and prodding to keep them moving.

They went up the stairs until they reached the ground floor. Assuming they were being taken to Lassigny's office, Will started to turn toward the big central staircase that led to the upper floors. Unexpectedly, Ramon stopped him.

"Not that way," he said. "Outside."

Will pushed the door open and led the way out into the courtyard. The storm clouds had cleared and the sunlight outside was bright and glaring—particularly for people who had spent the last two nights in the darkness of the cells. Maddie and Will shaded their eyes with their bound hands and hesitated, not sure where they were headed next.

"Northwest tower," Ramon ordered, pointing the way.

They crossed the bailey to the tower in the northwest corner, where Maddie had earned the wrath of a castle guard a few days prior, trying to get a closer look at the construction of the stone building. They made their way to the door and one of the guards moved ahead of them to open it, ushering the two prisoners inside.

"Stairs," Ramon told them, maintaining his monosyllabic instructions as he pointed his dagger toward the staircase in the center of the tower.

"Down?" Will asked, expecting that they were to be taken to another dungeon. But again, he was surprised by the answer.

"Up," Ramon told him, and Will shrugged and complied.

They wound their way up the staircase. Maddie counted eight floors as they went up, then they emerged onto a landing, where a corridor ran off to either side, lined with doors on the outer wall.

"Left," Ramon told them. "Third door."

They followed his directions. Will paused by the third door, waiting for instructions.

"Open it and go in," Ramon told him.

The two Rangers stepped into the room, followed by Ramon and the other guards. Will and Maddie studied their new surroundings. They were in what looked to be a small suite of rooms. Two wooden armchairs flanked a small fireplace along the outer wall. A small table and two straight-backed chairs were set opposite, next to the window. There were two bedrooms leading off the main sitting area, their entrances screened by heavy curtains. Will's and Maddie's belongings, including Will's mandola, had been collected from the sleeping niche they had used in the common room of the keep, and were stacked in the center of the sitting room.

Ramon swept a hand around the apartment. "Make yourself comfortable," he said. "The Baron will see you later."

He cut their hands free and gestured to the other guards, and they left the room, closing the door behind them. The two Rangers heard the click of the heavy lock being turned from the outside. Will and Maddie exchanged a puzzled look.

"Not what I'd expected," Will said.

Maddie shook her head and paced slowly around the room. In addition to the two bedroom areas, there was a third doorway, this one fitted with a door instead of curtains. She pushed it open and went in, finding herself in a small washroom, with a screened-off privy in one corner. She inspected that and found it to be clean and well maintained—a definite improvement on the facilities in Marius's dungeon cell. She went back to the main room, just as there was the rattle of a key in the lock and two servants entered the room. Outside in the corridor, two armed guards kept watch.

The servants glanced at the occupants of the room, then set down their burdens. One had a tray, covered with a white cloth.

The other carried a large bucket of hot water, steam rising from its surface. Hefting it awkwardly, he carried it to the washroom and deposited it on the floor, slopping a little of the hot water over the boards. The woman who had deposited the tray on the table removed the cloth cover to reveal soft rolls and a plate of sliced ham and cheese. Of greater interest to Will and Maddie, however, was the battered enamel pot, from which the fragrant scent of hot coffee wafted out. Maddie felt her mouth watering.

"Clean up, eat and drink," the male servant told them. "The Baron will send for you in an hour."

And with that, they withdrew from the room. Once more, a key clicked heavily in the outer lock. Will and Maddie exchanged another look.

"What's all this about?" Maddie asked.

Will shrugged. "Lassigny is sending us a message," he said. "He's going to want information from us. The dungeon showed us where we'll be if we don't give it to him. This is obviously where we'll be kept if we cooperate. It's the classic gilded cage, I'd say."

Maddie glanced meaningfully at the heavy timber door.

"But a cage, nevertheless," she said.

4

THEY HAD BATHED, EATEN AND CHANGED INTO FRESH CLOTH-
ing by the time Ramon returned to conduct them to their meeting with Lassigny. As before, he was accompanied by three
armed soldiers, and the two Rangers' hands were tied in front
of them before they left the suite of rooms.

"The Baron's waiting. Let's go," Ramon told them, leading
the way along the corridor.

They followed him down the stairs, with the three soldiers
behind them, their hands resting ready on the hilts of their daggers. The small party emerged into the courtyard and headed
for the keep. Word of their imprisonment had obviously gone
round the castle, and they were subjected to the curious stares of
those they passed.

As they entered the keep, Ramon gestured toward the wide
central stairway. "Upstairs," he told them, and they obeyed.

At the top of the first set of stairs, Will paused expectantly.
This was where the Baron's office was situated and he assumed
that was where they were heading. He was correct. Ramon, who
had followed them into the keep, moved past them and knocked
on the door leading to Lassigny's office.

After a few seconds, the door was opened by a balding, middle-aged man. Judging from his plain, unadorned work clothes, and the fact that he held a quill pen in his ink-stained fingers, Will took him to be a secretary or scribe working for the Baron.

"What is it?" the man asked. His disdainful manner indicated that he considered himself superior to common soldiers like Ramon, although it was doubtful that he would have shown such condescension if the Baron hadn't been close to hand.

"The prisoners are here, as the Baron ordered," Ramon told him. He seemed impervious to the scribe's supercilious manner. The balding man turned back into the room behind him.

"My lord, the pris—"

Lassigny's deep voice cut him off. "I heard, Nicolas. Bring them in."

The scribe opened the door wider and Ramon ushered his two charges into the room. He and the other guards followed close behind, fanning out to flank the prisoners.

Lassigny was seated in a high-backed wooden armchair behind the huge desk that faced the door. Its surface was strewn with papers and he held a sheet of parchment in one hand. A small, cushioned stool was in front of the desk—obviously where Nicolas had been sitting while he and the Baron were working. Lassigny beckoned him forward now and handed him the sheet.

"Take care of this," he said brusquely.

Nicolas took the paper from him and nodded his head in a bow. "Of course, my lord. Will that be all for now?"

"Yes. Get out of here and attend to all this nonsense." Lassigny waved his hand dismissively at the untidy pile of papers on the desk before him. Nicolas leaned forward and quickly gathered the pages together. Then, bowing obsequiously, he backed away toward the door, turning in the last few meters to hurry out and close the door behind him.

While all this was happening, Lassigny had fixed his dark, brooding eyes on the two figures standing before his desk. Now he switched his gaze to Ramon.

"Fetch chairs for them," he ordered. Ramon complied, pulling forward two straight-backed chairs from a half dozen that lined the walls of the room. He placed them in front of the desk, facing the Baron.

"Sit," Lassigny ordered the prisoners, and they complied. "Untie their hands," he said to Ramon, who gestured for one of the other men to untie Maddie while he attended to Will's bonds. Maddie massaged her wrists and flexed her fingers to aid the returning circulation. As ever, her fingertips had grown numb with the constriction of the rope. Lassigny seemed to be in no hurry to begin talking to them, and she glanced around the room while they waited.

The main item of furniture was the large table that the Baron used as a desk. Behind the Baron's chair was a life-size portrait of a nobleman who bore a distinct resemblance to Lassigny—an ancestor, she guessed. To one side of the painting, a pair of crossed halberds was mounted on the wall. On the other side was a shield bearing Lassigny's coat of arms—a stylized yellow hawk against a green background. To the right of the desk, on the right-hand wall, a large fireplace held a glowing log fire.

But it was an item to the left that took her attention. Resting against the wall was the long tubular case that had been hidden in the stall where Tug and Bumper were accommodated—a case that held Maddie's and Will's two bows and quivers full of arrows.

Lassigny, watching her intently with those black, depthless eyes, saw her notice the weapons case.

"Bring that here to me," he said to Ramon, indicating the case. When Ramon obeyed, Lassigny uncapped the tube and spilled the two bows and quivers out onto the surface of his desk. Ramon's eyebrows went up in surprise as he saw the weapons. The two saxes, in scabbards wound round with their belts, followed the bows, clattering heavily onto the tabletop. Ramon's surprised look intensified.

"Unusual belongings for a jongleur and his daughter, I would have thought," Lassigny said softly. He switched his gaze from Maddie to Will, as if expecting him to reply.

Will shrugged. "These are dangerous times, my lord," he said. "We're travelers and we need to be able to protect ourselves. The roads are full of perils and only a fool would go unarmed."

"Only a few days ago, in fact, we were accosted by robbers," Maddie put in, and Lassigny's eyes swung back to her, somewhat surprised that she had spoken up. He clearly expected Will, the older of the two and a male, to do the talking. Maddie sighed inwardly. It was an attitude with which she was familiar.

"Indeed, young lady?" he said. "And did you defend yourself with these fearsome weapons?"

He drew one of the arrows from its quiver, fingering the steel broadhead and testing the sharpness of its edges with his thumb.

"There was no need," she replied. "A passing warrior came to our aid and drove the bandits off."

"How very considerate of him," Lassigny said. "And what was his name?"

Maddie shrugged. "I've no idea, my lord. He rode off in pursuit of the bandits before we could ask him."

"What a shame," the Baron said sarcastically. Sarcasm seemed to be his standard manner, Maddie thought. He sat studying her, saying nothing, and she took the opportunity to take stock of him. Unlike Will, she had previously had little chance to appraise the Baron at close quarters, aside from a brief encounter in the courtyard some days ago.

He was dark-haired, although there were streaks of gray in the black, and his eyes, as she had noted, were like pieces of obsidian—black and impenetrable. His features were strong and regular. There was a small scar that showed white above his left eye, evidence of an old wound, she thought. His shoulders were broad, as might be expected in a man who had trained as a knight. As he was sitting behind the desk, it was difficult to assess his height. But she knew from the encounter in the courtyard that he was slightly taller than average.

The most significant aspect of the man was his attitude—the condescending, disdainful manner with which he addressed them, and anyone else he spoke to. He obviously believed in his own innate superiority and made no effort to hide the fact.

He finished his appraisal of her and turned quickly back to Will. His manner was abrupt and his movements were quick and darting, rather like the hawk portrayed on his coat of arms.

"You're Araluens," he said. As Will had noted on a previous encounter, the Baron liked to switch subjects quickly when he was questioning someone. It was a tactic designed to catch his subject off guard, and perhaps elicit an incautious answer.

"That's correct, my lord," Will said. There was little point in denying it. They had discussed this matter when the Baron had commanded Will to entertain his dining companions.

"So why are you working for Philippe?" the Baron asked.

Will spread his hands in a disingenuous gesture. "He offered to pay us, my lord," he said. "He offered to pay us well." His tone indicated that the answer was self-evident. But Lassigny stroked his short beard thoughtfully as he mulled over the answer.

"So you owe no particular allegiance to Philippe?" he asked.

Not *King Philippe*, Will noticed. Again, he shrugged. "We work for whoever pays us, my lord," he said. "We owe no particular loyalty to the King beyond that. As you pointed out, we're Araluens, not Gallicans."

Will suddenly sensed where this conversation might be going. Lassigny's next statement confirmed his suspicions.

"You're mercenaries, in fact—spies for hire." There was no sense in denying the statement. Essentially, it was the truth. Equally, there was no sense in agreeing. Will remained silent. Those dark eyes bored into him once more.

"So presumably," the Baron said, "you'd work for anyone who paid you well."

Will nodded. "I don't see why not."

"Interesting," the Baron said, at length. "We'll talk more on this." He turned to Ramon and snapped his fingers. "Take them back to the tower."

5

RAMON AND THEIR GUARDS ESCORTED THEM BACK ACROSS the courtyard to the northwest tower and then to their apartment. Once again, they heard the key turn in the lock as he closed the door behind him.

"What was all that about?" Maddie asked, once they were alone.

Will scratched his beard thoughtfully. "I'd say our friend may be trying to recruit us," he replied.

"Recruit us?" Maddie said. "For what purpose?"

"To gather information for him. After all, he's plotting and planning to overthrow the King—at least, that's what Anthony seems to think. And if he's doing that, he needs to know where the other barons and nobles stand."

"So he'd use us to travel around and pick up information for him?" Maddie asked.

He nodded. "It's possible that's what he's got in mind. After all, we're ideally suited to do it. It's relatively easy for us to gain access to castles and strongholds and his questions about our loyalty to Philippe were rather pointed. And describing us as mercenaries was equally so."

"I noticed you kind of fed that thought to him," she said. "Saying we'd work for whoever paid us."

"Was I that obvious?" Will asked.

She grinned. "Pretty much. You certainly didn't leave a lot of doubt."

"Well, it's fairly logical when you think about it. We're not Gallican, so we have no allegiance to the King. My guess is that he plans to spend the next few weeks sounding us out and winning us over." He paused. "There's something else too."

"And what might that be?"

"Lord Anthony also believed that Lassigny might have ambitions beyond the throne of Gallica. It's possible that he might be looking to attack Araluen in the long term. If that's the case, he may well want to pump us for information on Araluen's defenses."

"But we'd never tell him anything!" Maddie protested indignantly.

Will inclined his head. "Not intentionally. But if that is the case, he could well try to win us over. He'll become friendly and try to get us off guard. He'll offer to pay us well to work for him here in Gallica. And the more comfortable we become in that situation, the more he can learn from us. It's amazing how much you can give away when you let your guard down."

"But we're not planning on letting our guard down," Maddie said.

Will smiled at her. "No. But he doesn't know that. Remember, he thinks of us as mercenaries, as spies who work for money. My guess is he's going to try to gradually gain our trust, to get us working for him so that we relax a little around him. Then he'll try to get more and more information out of us. Men like

Lassigny tend to judge others by their own standards. He's prepared to betray his King and he assumes that other people will have the same lack of loyalty."

"So what do we do?" Maddie asked.

"We play him at his own game. We'll pretend to go along with him, and be willing to work for him if he suggests it. Mind you, he won't do it in a hurry. He'll work on getting us relaxed before he makes any sort of obvious move. So we'll bide our time, and maybe in the meantime we'll find a way out of here. Speaking of which . . ."

He'd been sitting on the edge of one of the chairs. Now he rose and walked to the window. There was no lock. It was fastened by a simple lever that dropped into a retaining latch. He lifted it now and pushed the window open, leaning out to check the surrounds. He drew back inside again, smiling.

"Take a look at this," he said.

Maddie joined him, craning out through the narrow opening. "What am I looking for?"

"The stonework. Take a good look at it."

She did as he suggested and saw that the stonework around the window had been freshly plastered. For a distance of two meters around the window—above, below and to either side—the rough irregularities and gaps in the stonework had been filled and smoothed over. There was no chance of a climber finding a handhold or foothold anywhere around the window.

Which meant they had no chance of climbing out and making their way down the tower.

"That makes it awkward," she said. In the back of her mind,

she had entertained the idea that, if they chose, they could climb down from their prison, much as they had scaled the tower to reach Prince Giles. Now it was clear that there was no way for them to leave, other than by the door.

The locked door.

"He's no fool," Will said. "He obviously worked out how we reached Giles. Maybe that's why they kept us in the dungeon for a couple of days. As well as sending us a none-too-subtle message—*this is what's waiting for you if you don't toe the line*—it gave them time to do this."

Maddie moved away from the window and sat at the table. She was frustrated by the fact that one possible avenue of escape had been effectively blocked.

"So what do we do?" she said again.

"We wait. We see what Lassigny has in mind. We let him work on getting us to lower our guard. My guess is we'll be seeing him regularly. He'll meet with us, talk with us and work on getting us to feel comfortable. I read a report last year about a strange phenomenon that occurs when a person is held prisoner for an extended time."

"What's that?"

"The prisoner begins to identify with their captor. They become dependent on them and, strangely, they begin to feel closer to them. They begin to trust them."

"That's crazy."

Will shrugged. "Maybe. Maybe not. Once captives realize there's no way they can escape, a sense of complacency begins to creep in. Their captor is, in a strange way, looking after them—providing food and shelter for them—and they become dependent on him. That could be what Lassigny is banking on."

"Well, he's going to be disappointed," Maddie said, with some energy.

"Maybe," Will told her. "But we won't let him know."

The sun dropped in the western sky and the shadows grew longer in the courtyard far below. As the sun eventually disappeared, Will and Maddie lit the lamps that had been provided. There was kindling and firewood by the side of the small fireplace, and Maddie prepared a fire and lit it. Soon, the warmth of the flames filled the room and they sat in armchairs on either side of the hearth. Will produced his mandola from its case and started quietly picking away at a tune. The melody was familiar to Maddie, and she took her gaze off the flames and glowing coals in the fireplace and looked at him.

"What's that song?" she asked.

He glanced up, his fingers continuing to find the correct notes as he played. "'La lune, elle est mon amour.' 'The moon is my love,'" he told her, then added, "It's the one Prince Louis asked me about when we were at Chateau La Lumiere."

"That's right," she said. "I thought I recognized it." The prince had sung a part of the song to them when he had asked Will if he knew it. "Where did you learn it?"

"I asked one of the servants in the main hall to sing it for me," he said. "I was going to add it to my repertoire, in spite of Lassigny's disparaging comment about my accent."

"It's pretty," she said. She settled back, eyes closed, to enjoy the music as Will continued to practice, rapidly becoming more and more adept at the song. She was somewhat envious of Will's playing. It gave him a way to pass the time, whereas she had nothing to distract her. She considered practicing her juggling but rejected the idea. It was warm by the fire, and she couldn't see any point in developing her skill with the juggling balls in the current circumstances. She shifted in her chair to make herself more comfortable and closed her eyes. Eventually she dozed off.

The rattle of the key in the lock roused her. She glanced around, wondering for a moment where she was, then remembering. The door opened and two servants came in, bearing covered trays, which they set on the table before exiting. Maddie caught a glimpse of the ever-present armed guards outside in the corridor before the door closed and the key turned once more.

They rose from their armchairs. Will set the mandola to one side, away from the heat of the fire, and they moved to the table.

"Let's see what's for dinner," he said.

The food was plain but plentiful and tasty. It consisted of a rich vegetable stew and fresh baked bread, still slightly warm in spite of traveling from the kitchens in the central keep to their tower room. Two apples were provided as a dessert.

Maddie didn't drink alcohol, and Will only imbibed sparingly. But he poured a small goblet and tasted the wine, letting it run round his mouth to develop its full flavor.

"Not bad," he said appreciatively. "Not bad at all. I'd say my theory is correct." He indicated the food and drink before them. "The Baron is trying to soften us up."

6

As time passed, it became increasingly apparent that this was precisely what Lassigny had in mind. The following day, they were served an equally appetizing breakfast of coffee, soft rolls, and sliced ham and cheese. Then, in the midmorning, Ramon arrived with his familiar entourage of armed guards and escorted them down to the terraced garden behind the keep.

"The Baron says you can stretch your legs and get some fresh air," he told them.

Will exchanged a meaningful glance with his apprentice. "Sounds like he's our new best friend," he said quietly.

They strolled through the flower beds and benches that were set around the garden, enjoying the sunshine. The guards formed a protective circle around them and it soon became obvious that, even if the Baron was planning to treat them well, there were still some restrictions. Nobody was allowed to approach or talk to them. Anyone who tried—and there were several who did, Will being well-known and well-regarded as an entertainer— were blocked off and hustled away by their guards. One household servant, bolder than the rest, questioned them from a distance as they passed.

"What are you in trouble for?" he called, but Ramon reacted quickly before either of them could speak.

"Don't answer that!" he snapped. Then, turning to the man who had posed the question, he said in a harsh tone, "And you keep your mouth shut. Move away!"

He dropped his hand threateningly onto the hilt of his short sword and the servant retreated quickly, hiding himself among the small throng strolling and taking the sun.

Maddie smiled. "It seems there are definite limits to our newfound freedom," she remarked.

They stopped by a fountain that bubbled cheerfully near the northern wall. It was surrounded by a low wall and a garden bed sown with white river rocks. Maddie sat on the lip of the wall and idly examined one of the rocks. It was smooth and rounded by the passage of river water over it. She tossed it casually in the palm of her hand.

It seemed an innocent enough gesture but there was a purpose to it. The rock was heavy and hard, being basically marble. And it was smooth and evenly formed. Will watched her as she glanced at Ramon. When she saw his attention was elsewhere, she slipped the rock into her pocket and picked up another, subjecting it to the same seemingly casual study, before pocketing it as well. She took another rock, turning it over in her hand like the others. But this one, she tossed idly back into the garden.

"No good?" Will asked quietly.

She shook her head. "Uneven. It wouldn't fly true."

He nodded. He had suspected what she was doing but her comment confirmed it. Her sling was wound in a diamond pattern around her belt, concealed in full view as an apparent piece of decoration on the belt. The leather pouch, which might have given away its true nature, was at the back, concealed from view by the belt itself.

She picked up another and discarded it after several seconds. Then she took a third and a fourth, surreptitiously adding them to the first two in her pocket. Will noticed that one of the other guards was watching her. His manner was casual and he didn't seem as if he was suspicious, but it never paid to take a chance.

"Don't overdo it. One of them is watching," Will said, craning his neck as if to watch a rook circling the keep tower high above them. He noticed that the guard also looked up to see what he was studying.

"I'll get more tomorrow," Maddie replied, equally casually. Then she rose and began to pace across the neatly trimmed grass of the garden. Will followed her and their escort moved with them, maintaining a loose cordon around them. A few minutes later, Ramon glanced at the position of the sun in the sky.

"Time to get back," he said, gesturing at the keep. Will turned reluctantly toward the tower that housed their prison—comfortable, certainly, but, as he had observed, no less a prison for that.

"You can come back tomorrow," Ramon told him. "Baron says you can get some fresh air every day if you want to."

"Maybe tomorrow we could stroll down to the village?" Will suggested innocently.

Ramon allowed himself a mirthless smile. "And maybe pigs can fly," he said.

They made their way back to the northwest tower. Just before they entered the tower, Maddie became conscious of eyes upon her. She turned quickly and scanned the garden. Some twenty meters away, she caught a glimpse of blue and white and saw the white-haired beggar, leaning heavily on a long staff, watching her. As Ramon stepped forward to chivvy her in through the door, the old man slipped away behind a knot of strolling kitchen servants.

"Keep moving!" Ramon ordered.

She turned back to the doorway. Her mind was racing. There was definitely something about the old man, but try as she might, she couldn't put her finger on it. Will, noticing her hesitate at the foot of the stairs, moved closer to her.

"What is it?" he asked quietly.

But she shook her head. "Nothing. I'm fine," she replied.

Then Ramon was ordering them to keep moving once more, and to stop talking, so she led the way up the winding stairway, hearing the guards' boots clattering on the stone behind her.

Back in their apartment, with the door firmly closed and locked behind them, she turned to Will. "That beggar: Did you notice him?"

He gave her a blank look and shook his head, puzzled. "What beggar?"

"Long white hair and beard. He's wearing a blue-and-white-striped cloak and carrying a staff," she said. But she could see by his expression that Will hadn't noticed the old man. She continued. "I've seen him before once or twice in the courtyard. There's something strangely familiar about him."

Will pondered her answer for several seconds, then replied, "Can't say I've noticed him. You say you've seen him before?"

She pursed her lips in frustration. "I'm not sure. He just seems . . . familiar somehow."

"Maybe he was in the audience at Entente?" he suggested.

Entente was the mountain village where they had performed before arriving at Falaise.

Maddie looked doubtful.

"I don't think so," she said. "I think I'd remember if he'd been there. It's so maddening!" she added. Then she shrugged off the frustration. "I guess it'll come to me if I don't think about it."

"That's usually the way it happens," Will agreed.

But of course, it was one thing to say she wasn't going to think about it, quite another to actually do so. She rummaged through her bag of clothes to find an old sock, which she used as a receptacle for the river stones she had collected.

But all the time, her thoughts went back to the old man in the blue-and-white cloak.

"Maybe he just reminds me of someone," she said to herself. But even that didn't do anything to allay her frustration.

"And if that's so," she muttered, "*who* is it he reminds me of?"

But, for the moment at least, the question would remain unanswered.

7

FOUR DAYS WENT BY WITH NO CHANGE TO THEIR ROUTINE. Each day, Ramon and his men would escort them to the garden at the rear of the bailey for fresh air and exercise. For the moment, there was no further contact with Lassigny.

"This is getting boring," Maddie said one afternoon, leaning her elbows on the windowsill, and peering out at the courtyard below them and the keep tower that faced them.

Will looked up from his mandola. He was now proficient playing the accompaniment to the Gallic love song that he had set out to learn, and had moved on to improvising an instrumental break. At least he had something to do to occupy his time, Maddie thought moodily.

Will set the instrument aside and stood, moving to join her at the window. The view from this elevated position was a good one. They could see over the southern wall with its fortified gatehouse opening onto the causeway and then the village. Beyond that, the forests and the hills rolled away from them into the distance. Seabirds and rooks soared on the air currents that swirled around the castle, and the ever-present sound of waves could be heard clearly as they crashed at the foot of the rocky outcrop that formed the basis for the building. The squat bulk of the keep tower dominated the foreground, and looking down, Will could make out the foreshortened figures of people moving in the courtyard and the grassed area on the northern side.

"That's quite a view," he said.

She grunted. "I've seen it. I see it every day and it never changes. It's boring. I'm bored. How are we going to get out of here?"

"Well, climbing is obviously not an option. I suppose we'll have to go out through the door."

"The door is locked," she said. "Maybe you hadn't noticed."

"True. But a lock can always be picked, can't it?"

"Can you pick a lock? This lock?"

He moved closer to the door and studied it. "Well, I could probably do it with a bent metal rod," he said. "Or a thick piece of wire."

Maddie looked around the room, searching for either item. Nothing sprang to view and she sighed.

"Or I could just use my lock picks," Will added, and she turned to him quickly.

"Where are they?" she asked.

"In my boot, where I normally keep them," Will replied.

Maddie grabbed his elbow and tried to drag him toward the door. "Well, come on, let's get this thing open!" she said.

But Will pulled back against her grip. "What, now?"

She nodded, pulling him with renewed energy. "Yes! Now! Let's get out of here!"

"How do we know there's not somebody outside?" he asked, and she hesitated. He continued. "I mean, it'd be a pity if there were half a dozen guards out there and they saw us come out. I'd lose my lock picks for a start, and that wouldn't be good. And besides, it's the middle of the day and there are people about. Where would we go? We'd be spotted immediately."

Maddie relaxed her grip on his arm as she saw the sense in what he was saying.

"That's true," she said. "Maybe we should wait till later tonight, when the castle's asleep."

"Or maybe we should give it a few more days," Will said, all traces of whimsy gone from his voice.

Maddie looked at him sharply. "Days?"

He nodded. "Or even a week," he said. "Maddie, I want to see if we can find out what the Baron has in mind. I suspect he's trying to get us on his side, to influence us and to make us relax. Sooner or later, he'll want to speak with us again and we'll get a better idea as to what he's planning. I suspect it's bigger than simply kidnapping Prince Giles and getting his hands on the adjoining province."

"I suppose you're right," she said glumly. "But why did you get me all excited with your talk about picking the lock?"

Will smiled gently at her. "You looked so downhearted. I wanted you to know that we do have a way out of here. It's just not the time to use it yet. And we'll need to make a plan. We need to figure out how to get out of the castle once we're out of this tower."

"Well, that shouldn't be too hard. We could just find a spot and go over the wall," Maddie said dismissively.

"And would Tug and Bumper climb over with us as well? Or did you plan on leaving them behind?"

Maddie sagged into the chair facing him, her enthusiasm deflating like a pricked balloon. "Oh . . . ," she said. "That's right." In her eagerness to be away, she had forgotten about their horses, currently accommodated in the castle stables. It would be difficult, to say the least, to sneak out of the castle with them. And naturally, she had no intention of leaving them behind. She looked at him shamefaced.

"I'd sort of forgotten about them," she admitted, and he nodded slowly.

"So we need to figure out a way to get them out with us. And in the meantime, we sit tight and wait till Lassigny wants to talk to us again."

The summons came two days later. They heard the sound of heavy boots in the corridor outside, then the key rattled in their door and Ramon opened it, stepping into the room. His ever-present guards could be seen in the background.

"Make yourselves presentable tonight," he ordered abruptly. "The Baron says you'll be dining with him."

Will raised his eyebrows. "Really? How kind of him. Tell him we'd be delighted to accept his invitation."

Ramon scowled at the joking tone. Humor wasn't his strong point. "It's not an invitation. It's an order."

Will made a moue, nodding thoughtfully several times. He looked at Maddie. "Does one accept an order to dinner?" he asked.

Maddie shrugged. "I think one complies," she said.

Ramon shook his head irritably. "Whether you accept or comply or not, you'll be dining with him. So make yourselves ready."

"Very well," said Will. "Any idea what's on the menu?"

"How would I know? I don't get to dine with the Baron very often. For all I know, you'll be eating larks' tongues in aspic and honey-coated grasshoppers."

Will appraised the soldier with a little more interest. Maybe he was wrong about Ramon lacking a sense of humor, he thought. Of greater importance was the fact that, as they were talking, Will had moved slightly to gain a better view of the corridor outside the room. He could see only the three guards who always accompanied Ramon. Apparently, there was no longer anyone stationed permanently outside their door. That was a useful piece of knowledge, in the light of his and Maddie's previous conversation.

"We'll come and collect you at the eighth hour," Ramon continued. "Make sure you're ready."

And so saying, he turned and left the room, locking the door behind him.

8

DINNER WAS SERVED IN THE SMALL DINING ROOM IN THE Baron's private apartment, not in the large hall where Will had entertained the knights and nobles who served under Lassigny. The Baron's wife joined them, along with one of Lassigny's senior knights.

"This is Armand," Lassigny said, by way of introduction. "He's the commander of the castle garrison."

Armand nodded disdainfully in their direction. He was in his mid-thirties, with long, dark-blond hair falling to his shoulders. His beard was trimmed short and his blue eyes were keen and alert. His full-lipped mouth was set in a petulant sneer as he studied them. Will couldn't remember seeing him in the audience or at the head table when he had performed for Lassigny some days prior. Perhaps he'd been on duty then, he thought.

Armand made no effort to disguise his frank perusal of the two Araluens. Maddie thought his open curiosity was verging on the side of rudeness. Her opinion was confirmed when he turned slightly to Lassigny.

"What are they called?" he asked.

Lassigny gestured for Will to answer the question.

"I'm Will Accord," he said, "and this is my daughter, Madelyn. You can call her Maddie if you choose."

Armand stared at him rudely for several seconds. "I think not," he said at length. He looked back at the Baron. "Why are these people dining with us?"

The Baron signaled to his senior servant to have the meal brought in. "They're going to tell us about Araluen," he said evenly.

Armand opened his mouth to reply but was forestalled by the arrival of the meal.

Three serving girls, supervised by the Baron's head servant, hurried to place platters on the table—a smoking pork loin roast with crisp, crackling skin and a tangy apple sauce, along with vegetables and a salad of chickpeas and finely sliced red onions in a sharp vinegar dressing. The long, crusty loaves of bread that seemed to be part of every Gallic meal nestled in several baskets, kept warm by white cloths.

For several minutes, further conversation was interrupted as the food was carved and served onto their platters. The head servant poured wine for the diners. Will signaled that he would have a glass. Maddie opted for water, clear and cold from the spring in the palace courtyard.

He's certainly not starving us, she thought, as she savored her first few mouthfuls of the tender, delicious pork. She cut off a piece of the light, crisp crackling. It flew apart in her mouth and she made a small noise of appreciation.

She glanced across the table at Will, who was opposite her. He tilted his head in appreciation of the food and gave a small shrug. She remembered his theory that Lassigny was trying to lull them into a sense of comfort.

Lull away, she thought. I can stand a lot of this.

Lassigny noticed her reaction and leaned forward to speak to her. "You enjoy our cuisine?" he asked.

She nodded. "Very much. Your chefs are very skillful." She helped herself from a cruet of apple sauce, spooning it generously over the pork on her platter.

He gave a short laugh. "Mine certainly are," he said. "I'm not sure about the rest of the country. What is Araluen food like?"

She cocked her head to one side, thinking about her answer. "It's quite hearty," she said. "Simpler than this and with stronger flavors. We eat more beef and mutton than pork."

"Do the common people eat beef and mutton?" Lady Lassigny asked, injecting herself into the conversation for the first time.

"Not at every meal. We eat meat perhaps three times a week. The other days, we eat vegetables—potatoes, carrots, turnips. Corn is popular."

Will smiled to himself, noting how Maddie included herself with the common people, dispelling any thought that she might be of noble birth. She was no fool, he thought.

"Does Araluen have a large army?" Lassigny asked. His tone was casual and he seemed to be totally engrossed in the slice of pork he was carving.

There it is again, Will thought. The sudden change of topic that might trick you into an unguarded reply.

But Maddie's expression was blank. "I think my father is better able to answer that question. I'm just a girl, after all," she said, smiling demurely.

Armand snorted quietly, obviously agreeing with her.

Lassigny turned to direct the question at Will. "Well?" he asked. "Tell us about the Araluen army."

"They don't have a large standing army," Will replied, choosing the pronoun to disassociate himself from the Araluen establishment. "Each of the fiefs maintains a battleschool."

"Fiefs?" Lassigny queried. "What are these fiefs?"

"Similar to your baronies. There are fifty of them, some larger than others. Each one is presided over by a baron. The battleschools train young men to become knights and men-at-arms. They provide a basic force of skilled warriors. If more are needed, the king can raise levies from the general population."

"Untrained troops?" Lassigny mused.

Will shrugged. "Not really. The battleschools are also tasked with training the levies. They hold camps throughout the year to teach them their skills. They train them with pikes, spears and close weapons. The levies provide the basic infantry that might be needed."

And archers, Will thought. But he felt it might be better to let Lassigny find out about them for himself. Araluen law required the young men of every village to practice regularly with the longbow, providing a ready source of thousands of trained archers in the event of war or invasion.

"I see," said the Baron thoughtfully. "So your country has a small but professional army. When was it last called upon to protect the realm?"

"Quite recently," Will said. "There was a rebellious cult that sprang up. They disagreed with the law of female succession."

Armand leaned forward. "And what, precisely, is that?"

"It's the law that says a daughter can inherit the throne from her father if there is no male heir older than she is," Will explained.

Armand's lip curled. "Ridiculous," he muttered. "Women have no place ruling."

Maddie, watching closely, noticed that Lassigny's wife turned a disparaging look on the knight. Apparently she didn't share his antipathy toward women ruling a country.

Will shrugged the comment aside. "You may think so. But it's the law, nonetheless. The rebellion was quickly put down. Many of the dissidents were mercenary troops from Sonderland."

Lassigny nodded thoughtfully, filing the information away. Then, abruptly, he turned to Maddie. "Tell me about the Araluen Rangers," he said.

Earlier that day, Will had warned Maddie about Lassigny's trick of suddenly switching subjects during a conversation—or, more accurately, an interrogation.

Maddie replied calmly, without seeming to be perturbed by the question.

"There's not a lot to tell," she said. "They're foresters employed by the King. They patrol the woods and forests, protecting the King's deer from poachers."

It was the Ranger Corps's standard answer to queries from outsiders, and Maddie had learned it in her early days as an apprentice. It served to make the Corps seem relatively harmless and unimportant, and to preserve the secrecy that shrouded them.

But Lassigny wasn't satisfied. "I'd heard they are warriors," he said bluntly.

Now Will intervened in the conversation. "Warriors? Not at all, my lord. They're simple woodsmen. They are armed with longbows, of course. But that's more for hunting than warfare."

The dark eyes swung back to Will. "And I'd heard you were one of them," he challenged.

But Will laughed the suggestion aside. "Hardly, my lord. I

enjoy my creature comforts too much to go skulking off through the forests keeping tabs on deer. I prefer to see them on the table in front of me, roasted and seasoned."

"And yet you carry a longbow?" Lassigny seemed unconvinced.

"It's not an uncommon weapon in Araluen, my lord," Will explained. "Particularly for someone like me, who is unskilled with the sword."

"And how skillful are you with the bow?" Lassigny prompted.

Will seemed to consider the question for several seconds, then answered. "I suppose I'm adequate," he said. It was not something that Lassigny could test, after all. If he asked for a demonstration, it would be easy for Will to conceal his ability.

"I suppose your real skill lies in spying and gathering information," Lassigny said—another jump to a new subject.

Will made a dissembling gesture with both hands spread. "Not so skillful, my lord. After all, it didn't take you long to uncover us."

Lassigny smiled for the first time that evening. "Aaah, but that's no reflection on your abilities. We knew about you before you arrived."

Will and Maddie exchanged a surprised look. Maddie tilted her head, signaling for Will to pursue the statement. By now, in spite of Lady Lassigny's earlier reaction to Armand, she was familiar with the disdain that Lassigny and his subordinate felt for the female point of view.

"You knew about us, my lord?" Will asked.

Lassigny waved a dismissive hand in the air. "Not your actual identities, of course. But we knew there were spies coming here from Araluen. You were betrayed, you see," he added, with a superior smile. "Happens all the time in this country."

Will's eyes narrowed. "May I ask who betrayed us, my lord?" he asked, the hostility evident in his voice.

Lassigny shook his head indulgently. "Think about it, jongleur," he said. "There were at least a dozen people who accompanied Philippe on his 'secret' trip to Araluen." He paused as Maddie and Will exchanged another surprised glance. "Oh yes, I know all about that. It's *very* hard to keep secrets in Gallica, as I said. It could have been any one of them." He paused as the head servant coughed discreetly to gain his attention.

"But now, enough of this talk of spies and traitors, fascinating though it may be," he said. "Gaston has just indicated that our dessert is ready. We'll discuss this more another time."

9

"So who could the traitor be?" Maddie asked, once Ramon had left them alone in their apartment.

Will shook his head. "As Lassigny said, it could be any of the men who accompanied Philippe to Araluen. They'd have to be the most likely suspects."

"Except for his brother, Louis," Maddie said. "After all, he's family. He'd hardly betray his own brother."

"Perhaps. But at this stage, I wouldn't discount anyone. Gallicans are strange people."

Maddie paused, her forehead wrinkled in concentration. "Or it might be no one from that group. It might be someone from Chateau La Lumiere who found out about us. The Baron may well have thrown out the suggestion that it was one of the men who accompanied Philippe to throw us off the scent."

They sat in silence for a minute or so, thinking over the events of the night. Then Maddie spoke again.

"What I don't get is why he told us in any case. Why let us know that someone betrayed us?"

"It's all part of his plan," Will said. "He wants to slowly bring us over to his side. He wants us to feel comfortable and at ease—members of his inner circle. Sharing information like that is part of the process."

"I guess so. I see what you meant about the way he jumps from one topic to another to keep us off balance," she said.

Will smiled at her. "You handled it well," he said. "But perhaps it's time we started to give him some of his own medicine—time to get him a little off balance."

"How would we do that?" Maddie asked.

"We feed him information he isn't expecting."

"About what?" Maddie asked.

A conspiratorial grin spread over Will's face. "He wants information about the Rangers. Maybe we'll start to give him some—but more than he's expecting. That could definitely get him off balance. Besides," he added, "I'd like to create a worm of doubt in his mind in case Anthony's right."

"About what?" Maddie asked.

"About the idea of attacking Araluen if he can usurp Philippe. I'd like to get him thinking that it might not be as easy as he thinks."

The beggar in the blue-and-white-striped cloak was slumped against the keep wall to one side of the stairs leading up to the main door. He huddled against the rough stone, his ragged cloak clutched around him to ward off the chill night air. Beside him, the long staff he used for balance was propped against the wall.

A foot patrol of two soldiers noticed him sleeping there. They were familiar with the ragged old man—they had seen him in the bailey quite often. The senior of the two, a middle-aged man, was content to let the old fellow lie there, even though the rules said all day visitors had to be out of the castle grounds by sundown, when the main gate closed. But the younger patrolman was more inclined to enforce the rules strictly. He wasn't sure if his companion was testing him, seeming to ignore the old beggar to see if his young companion would do the same—at which time he would deliver a blistering lecture on the need for constant vigilance. Accordingly, he approached the figure and prodded him with the butt of his halberd.

"Oy! You! Wake up!"

The old beggar stirred at the rough touch. He looked up through bleary eyes, uncertain as to where he was.

"Eh? What? Wassamatter?" he mumbled.

"Let him alone. He's harmless," said the middle-aged guard.

But the young man prodded again. "Rules are rules," he told his companion stiffly. Then he addressed the beggar. "You! Get up! You can't doss down here for the night! Get moving!"

Grumbling under his breath, the white-haired old man struggled to his feet, swaying uncertainly.

"Not doin' any harm," he complained. "Why can't you let a man sleep?"

"You're not allowed to stay here," the younger guard told him, prodding him toward the main gate with his halberd. "Come on. Back to the village. We'll have to let you out the wicket gate."

Still half asleep and moving unsteadily, the beggar allowed himself to be herded toward the gatehouse, retrieving his staff and leaning heavily on it as he hobbled along between his two escorts. He continued to mutter complaints and insults under his breath as the indignant guard shoved him with the shaft of the halberd. The older guard smiled to himself as he made out the words "officious little popinjay" among the beggar's mumbling. It was a pretty fitting description of his companion, he thought.

They escorted him to the gatehouse, where one of the gate guards greeted them.

"Why, it's old Tomkin," he said cheerfully. "What are you doing still in the castle?"

The beggar muttered incoherently. The guard could vaguely make out the words "trying to get a night's sleep" among his grumbling.

"Well, you can't do that in the castle," the guard told him. "You should be back in the village by now. Should have been there hours ago," he added. He seized old Tomkin by the arm to lead him to the wicket gate. He was a little surprised when he did. He'd expected the beggar's arm to be thin and emaciated. Instead, he found himself gripping a firm, hard-muscled arm. He looked at the old man in some surprise.

"You're not as feeble as you look, are you, my friend," he said.

Tomkin shrugged the hand away and allowed himself to be led to the wicket gate—a small door set into the larger main gate, which allowed entry and exit when the castle was locked down. He stooped to go through it, although he wasn't a tall man, and shuffled away from the castle, hearing the wicket gate close and lock behind him. Using his staff to maintain his balance, the beggar crossed the narrow causeway and set off for the village, several hundred meters downhill. His staff tap-tapped on the hard-packed dirt road as he made his way toward the village. Behind him, the three guards watched his progress through a small viewing port, fitted with an iron grille.

"Where does he sleep?" the older patrolman asked idly. His young partner shrugged but the gate guard answered.

"People probably let him bed down in their barns or stables," he said. "He's quite harmless."

"We could have let him sleep in the courtyard," the patrolman said.

But his young companion stiffened, sensing criticism. "Rules are rules," he said.

The other two exchanged a glance, the gate guard raising an eyebrow.

The younger man saw the expression and his face reddened slightly. "Rules are rules," he repeated, in a firmer tone.

His companion jerked his thumb toward the courtyard. "Time we were back on patrol," he said.

Tomkin continued to shuffle down the hill. At the bottom of the slope, where the first of the homes and shops began to line either side of the road, he paused and glanced back up at the castle. There was no sign that anyone was watching him still, so he turned and continued on down the high street, where the buildings became more numerous and more closely spaced.

At this time of night, there was nobody about. The villagers were all inside their homes, close by the fire or in bed. As he continued on, a strange transformation came over him. He stood more erect, no longer bent over, and his shuffling, uncertain gait turned into a firm stride. The staff swung in a wider arc, clacking on the road in a sharp rhythm as he moved more quickly. Halfway down the high street, he turned off to the right, into a narrow lane that led away from the center of the village. The houses were smaller here and more densely packed together. Narrow alleys separated them, barely wide enough for a man to pass down them, leading to the rear yards where the householders kept vegetable gardens and chickens.

He passed half a dozen of these mean little dwellings before he stopped outside one. Glancing round, he checked the lane in either direction, then, stooping under the low-hanging eaves of the thatched roof, pulled on a length of twine attached to the latch inside the door.

He heard the wooden latch scrape out of the retaining bracket and pushed the door open, closing it quickly behind him as he entered.

The house consisted of one room, with a fireplace taking up one wall and two narrow beds at the other end. In between was a rough table and three crudely fashioned stools. The floor was packed dirt, strewn with rushes. A second door led out to the small yard behind the house, where a lean-to stable was situated, built onto the house. As Tomkin moved to warm himself by the fire, this door opened and a tall, broad-shouldered figure entered. Before the door closed, Tomkin heard a low-pitched whuffle of greeting from the stable and the clomping sound of a horse stamping its foot.

"Any luck?" asked the tall man, but Tomkin shook his head.

"The guards won't let anyone get near them," he said. "I had no chance to make contact. But at least I found out what room they're in."

The tall man moved to the fireplace and unhooked a black-ened coffeepot from a swiveling arm that suspended it over the flames. He poured a mug and offered it to Tomkin, who took it eagerly and drank deeply.

"Where are they?" asked his companion.

"They're in a room at the top of the northwest tower, facing into the courtyard. They were taken to see Lassigny tonight so I pretended to miss the gate closing. I waited till the guards took them back to the tower and saw the light go on in the top-floor room. Then I saw Maddie looking out the window."

"I wondered where you'd got to," the tall man said.

Tomkin took his coffee to the table and sat on one of the stools. "I'd better lie low for a couple of days," he said. "Two of the guards caught me in the bailey after the curfew. I had to pretend I was sleeping and they ran me out of the castle. The young one was the suspicious type so I might stay clear of the castle until things calm down. I don't want them paying too much attention to me."

His companion nodded. "You're hard to miss with that mass of white hair."

Tomkin ran the fingers of his free hand through his long, tangled hair. "Can't wait for this whole thing to be over. This mop of hair is driving me crazy. As soon as we're out of here, I'll be cutting it off."

The tall man grinned. "Presumably you'll use your saxe knife, as usual?"

"I'll use anything I can get my hands on," the beggar said ruefully, scratching away.

The tall man's grin widened. "Well, it'll be nice to have you back to your normal self, Halt," he said.

10

HALT WAS A SENIOR RANGER AND A MEMBER OF THE KING'S inner circle of advisers, which meant that he was a frequent visitor to Castle Araluen. Accordingly, a room was maintained for his use in an upper floor of the keep tower.

He had arrived at the castle late the previous night, in response to a summons from Gilan. After making his presence known to the Ranger Commandant, Halt went to his room and slept soundly. He rose early, as was his habit, and had breakfast in the main dining room of the keep—crispy bacon on toasted flatbread and a pot of excellent coffee. He rolled up his napkin and placed it on his crumb-strewn platter, then took a final sip of coffee, smacking his lips with relish.

As Halt was rising from the table, Horace entered the dining room, looked round and saw him. The tall knight made his way down the long trestle table where Halt had been sitting, and reached out to grasp his right forearm in greeting.

"Halt! Good to see you. They told me you arrived late last night," he said.

The Ranger nodded. "It was close to midnight, so I didn't bother you. I reported in to Gilan and then turned in. Gilan says the King wants to talk to us. What's it about?"

Horace shrugged. "He hasn't told me yet. But I suspect it has to do with Will and Maddie's mission in Gallica."

"Have they left yet?" Halt asked. "I heard Maddie needed some extra training for the job."

"That's right. She was working with one of the entertainers here. But she's finished that and they left last week. The King's worried about them."

"Well, let's go talk to him and maybe we'll find out what he wants," said Halt, and they walked briskly out of the dining room, heading for the stairs that would take them to Duncan's office.

There were two spearmen guarding the double doors to the King's room. They recognized the Ranger and the commander of the Araluen army—both were well-known figures in the castle. Even so, one of the guards held up a hand for them to stop.

"Just a moment please, sirs," he said, an apologetic tone in his voice. Horace nodded easily, unoffended by his action. It was the guard's duty to stop and announce any visitors to the King's office, no matter how important they might be.

"Announce us, please, Bedford," Horace told him.

Halt smiled as he saw the slight start of surprise from the guard at the fact that the army commander knew his name. Halt was willing to bet that Horace knew *all* his troops by sight and most of them by name. It was part of being a good leader and commander, and Horace was one of the best.

Bedford turned and rapped his knuckles on the door and

waited until he heard a muffled voice from inside, giving permission to enter. He turned the door handle on the left-hand door and eased it open a meter, putting his head around to speak to the King.

"Sir Horace and the Ranger Halt are here, sir," he said.

"Tell them to come in," said Duncan from within.

Bedford pushed the door open farther and stepped to one side, allowing Halt and Horace to pass by him and enter the office. He closed the door behind them after they had entered.

Duncan rose from his seat behind the huge desk to greet them. Halt noted that Duncan winced slightly as he put his weight on his injured leg—it tended to stiffen if he sat in one place too long. But the grimace was quickly replaced by a warm smile of greeting.

"Welcome back, Halt," he said. "It was good of you to come so quickly."

Halt allowed a slight smile to cross his normally grim features. There were few kings who would thank a subject for coming quickly in response to a summons. But Duncan was one of them, and his gratitude was genuine.

"Gilan suggested there was some urgency involved, sir," he said.

Duncan waved them to seats and lowered himself back into his own chair, grunting slightly as he eased the weight off his leg.

"Yes," he said. "We don't have a lot of time. I want you to go to Gallica for me."

Halt and Horace exchanged a quick glance. After Horace's earlier comments, the order didn't come as a complete surprise. But it was an unusual one.

"With Will and Maddie, sir?" Halt asked.

But Duncan shook his head. "No. They left several days ago. They'll be well on their way to Chateau La Lumiere by now. I want you to go directly to Chateau des Falaises."

Halt opened his mouth to ask a question but Duncan forestalled him. "It's Baron Lassigny's castle," he explained. "Will and Maddie will be heading there once they've met with King Philippe and got his final instructions. I want you to be there ahead of them."

"I assume that's where Lassigny is holding the King's son hostage?" Halt said.

Duncan nodded, fiddling with a narrow-bladed stiletto he kept on his desk as a paper knife. "That's our best guess," he replied. "It's the obvious place, after all. According to Anthony, it's a pretty formidable fortress." Lord Anthony was the King's chamberlain, and the head of his secret service network of agents and spies.

"So you want the two of us to besiege this castle and capture it," Halt said with a wry smile.

Duncan shook his head. "No. I want you to go quite peaceably and discreetly," he said. "I just want you to be on hand there in case Will and Maddie run into any trouble."

"I'll be glad to do it," Horace said. "After all, she is my daughter. But this is a little unusual, isn't it? Will knows what he's doing and Maddie is pretty capable as well—she proved that during the Red Fox rebellion."

It wasn't normal practice for the Rangers to send extra people on a mission like this. After all, there was an old saying that went "one riot, one Ranger." And there were already two Rangers on this mission, Horace thought. Duncan was nodding before Horace finished the question.

"Normally, I'd agree with you," he said. "And I take the point that Maddie is your daughter. She's also my granddaughter, and the second in line to the throne. But it's more than that."

He paused and the two men waited for him to elaborate. Finally, he did so, with a certain reluctance.

"I don't completely trust Philippe," he said after several seconds.

Halt sensed the distaste Duncan felt at having to pass that judgment on his fellow king. Duncan himself was an honorable man. He believed that a king should be totally dependable and above any sort of deceit and double-dealing. Philippe, sad to say, didn't live up to those same high ideals.

"I can't say I blame you, sir," Halt said quietly.

Duncan sighed and raised his eyebrows. "It's just a feeling I have about the man. His own court is a hotbed of intrigue and skulduggery—the Gallic court always has been like that. I have the sense that he'll be happy to use Maddie and Will to suit his own purposes but, if the worst comes to the worst, he'll leave them hanging in the wind."

"He didn't strike me as the most trustworthy person I've ever met," Horace put in. "And, according to Anthony, he was rather disrespectful about you, sir."

Duncan shrugged. "That may be. It doesn't really bother me, although it's a strange attitude for someone who came here asking for help. I suppose I resented feeling obliged to help him. He played on the fact that kings have to stick together."

"Although, as Anthony pointed out, sir, it's possibly in our best interests to keep him on the throne," Horace replied.

Halt shot him a look, surprised by the sentiment. "Why's that?"

"He's the devil we know," Horace told him. "And he doesn't have the backing of enough of his nobles to mount a serious challenge to Araluen."

"Whereas this Lassigny might, if he managed to usurp him?" Halt asked, and the other two men nodded.

"Precisely," the King said. "And that's another reason why I resented having to help him. It seems wrong somehow to use our people to keep a weak king on his own throne. But that's the position he put me in," he said angrily. "I hate politics!"

"So, what do you want us to do exactly, sir?" Halt asked.

Duncan shook his head in frustration. "Exactly? I'm not sure. I just want you to be on hand in case Will and Maddie need someone to back them up. In case there's something we haven't considered. If you leave in the next few days and go straight to Chateau des Falaises, you should get there before Will and Maddie. Just keep an eye on them and make sure there's no problem we haven't foreseen. I'd like to know there's help close by in case they need it."

"Should we go to the castle itself, sir?" Horace asked.

Duncan considered the question, then shook his head. "I think not. Too many foreigners arriving in a short period might alert suspicion. The village of Falaise is close by the chateau. See if you can find somewhere to stay there. Rent a house for a few weeks. You can pose as a traveling knight and his serving man."

"Which one am I?" Horace asked, with a grin. Halt flashed a sardonic glance at him and Duncan deigned not to answer.

"Should we conceal the fact that we're Araluens, sir?" Halt asked.

"I think that would be wise. Halt, you can pose as a Hibernian—"

"I *am* a Hibernian, sir," Halt replied. Duncan smiled for the first time in their conversation. Now that he had crystallized his fears and was able to set a backup plan in motion, he was feeling less despondent.

"And, Horace, maybe you could pose as an itinerant Teutlandic knight. Do you speak any Teutlandic?"

"Nein, Herr King. But I do an eggsellent Teutlandic accent ven I speak der Common Tongue," Horace replied, stiffening and clicking his heels together. Both Duncan and Halt regarded him without speaking for several long seconds.

"What was that?" Halt asked, one eyebrow raised.

Horace, unabashed, grinned at him. "Dot vas my eggsellent Teutlandic accent."

"Perhaps you should do the talking, Halt," Duncan suggested.

Horace dropped the playacting and asked in his normal voice, "One thing more, sir: Should we let Maddie and Will know we're watching?"

Again, Duncan considered the question before answering. "Only if it becomes necessary. Otherwise, don't make any contact with them. You might be seen and it could raise suspicions."

"So, watch without being seen and be ready to help if there's trouble," Halt said, summing up their instructions.

"Exactly," Duncan told him. "I must say, I feel a lot better about this whole affair now I know you two will be on hand if needed." He chose not to look at the downside of the situation. This way, four of his best people would be involved in an operation that had a lot of question marks hanging over it. "When can you leave?" he added.

Horace exchanged a look with Halt. "Sooner the better, I think. If we can be in place before Will and Maddie arrive we'll have become part of the scenery and less likely to cause interest."

Halt nodded agreement. "So, tomorrow at first light?"

"Tomorrow at first light," Horace confirmed. He grinned at the shorter man. "The two of us in Gallica. Be like old times, Halt."

Halt's eyebrow went up again. "Oh, I do hope not," he said.

11

HALT AND HORACE MADE A FAST PASSAGE TO GALLICA. THEY set out at dawn the following morning and rode at a steady canter to the east. Reaching the coast and the small harbor town of Tilmouth, they found the Skandian duty ship, *Wolftail*, moored at the quay.

"Good," said Horace. "I'd hoped we'd find her in port and not on patrol. She'll be faster than any cargo ship we might be able to hire."

They rode down the stone quay to where the ship lay. As they approached, a burly figure climbed up onto the bulwarks of the ship, steadying himself on a stay, and watched them coming.

"Good afternoon, Jens," Horace called when they were close enough for easy conversation. In his capacity as commander of the army, he had met the skirl, as Skandians called their ship captains, several times.

The Skandian waved cheerfully. "Good day to you, Sir Horace," he said. Like most skirls, he possessed a booming voice that could be heard above the roaring waves and howling wind of a storm at sea.

"Glad we caught you in port. We need to get to Gallica, as

soon as possible," Horace called, reining in his battlehorse, Stamper. The duty ship was provided by Skandia each year and, in addition to anti-piracy and antislavery patrols, was at the disposal of the King and his senior officers who might need transport.

Jens waved a hand toward the ship. "Well, climb down off those nags and come aboard. We came in two days ago to restock on food and water. We were due to go out on patrol again tomorrow so it's lucky you caught us. I take it you're in a hurry?" Experience told him that the King's officers were *always* in a hurry.

Horace nodded. "I'd like to get away as soon as possible," he said.

The two riders dismounted and Jens called to his crew to see about loading the horses on board. He shook hands with Horace and eyed his companion curiously. Halt wasn't wearing his usual Ranger outfit. He was dressed in dull brown woolen trousers and a jerkin that reached down to mid-thigh, gathered at the waist by a heavy belt that carried his double knife scabbard. His massive longbow had been resting across his thighs as he rode. Now, he slung it over his left shoulder.

Noticing the look Jens gave him, Horace made the introductions. "Jens Wavechaser, this is my friend Halt," he said.

Jens became even more interested when he heard the name. "Halt?" he said. "Aren't you the Ranger who—"

"Threw up in your Oberjarl's helmet?" Halt cut in. "That's me."

In fact, Halt was a well-respected figure in Skandia. Years before, he had organized and led the defense against an invading Temujai army, stopping them at the outskirts of the capital, Hallasholm, and driving them back to their own lands. He had also, in fact, thrown up in Oberjarl Erak's helmet during a bout of seasickness—a malady to which he was prone. That story was equally well-known among the Skandians, and Jens grinned now as he recalled it.

"I'll warn the crew about you," he said. "Some of the younger ones may not have heard that story."

"Wavechaser?" Halt said. "That's an unusual name. How did you come by it?"

He knew that Skandian names were often the result of interesting deeds or habits. A name like Wavechaser promised to have a good story behind it.

Jens shrugged. "When I was a lad I used to ride the surf in a small one-man skiff," he replied.

Halt raised his eyebrows. "Can you swim?" he asked. He knew that most sailors couldn't.

Jens shook his head cheerfully. "Not a stroke," he admitted.

"Then you must have been good at chasing waves," Halt said.

"I was passable. The possibility of drowning adds a certain zest to the sport. You get better at it quickly. Or you don't get better at anything."

Horace shook his head. Skandians were known for their casual approach to life-threatening situations. He glanced at the ship, where some of the crew were rigging a derrick at the foot of the mast to hoist the horses onboard. Others were removing the hatches that covered the shallow well in the center of the ship where the horses would travel, held securely in canvas slings under their bellies that would support their weight and prevent them thrashing about and falling as the ship rolled and pitched.

"Take Abelard first," Halt said to the working party, indicating his small, shaggy horse. "He's done this before, and if this big brute of a battlehorse sees that he isn't panicked, it might help keep him calm."

While the horses were hoisted aboard—Stamper showing some signs of concern, with his ears flattened to his head and his big square teeth bared—Jens sent the ship's boy to fetch several bales of hay from the town.

"Be good for them to have something in their bellies," Jens observed, glancing through the gap in the breakwater, where the sea heaved in a succession of steep, short rollers.

Halt followed his gaze and pursed his lips in resignation. "I'd rather not think about that," he said, stepping down gingerly into the wolfship and staggering slightly as she moved beneath his feet on the small waves that found their way through the breakwater. Horace and Jens exchanged grins, with the usual sense of superiority and lack of sympathy from those who didn't suffer from seasickness for those who did.

"I think I'll sit down at the back," Halt said.

"Stern," Jens corrected him.

Halt turned a baleful eye on the skirl. "Whatever."

Jens turned back to Horace as the tall knight stepped lightly aboard. "So where in Gallica are you headed?"

Horace pointed to the northeast. "Take us northeast. I want to go ashore above the latitude of Chateau La Lumiere."

Jens nodded thoughtfully, drawing up a mental picture of the Gallican coast. "Have you got any particular port in mind?"

But Horace shook his head. "No port. I don't want to be seen arriving. Set us down on a deserted beach somewhere. Is that possible?" he added. He wasn't a sailor but he knew that sometimes it could be dangerous to approach an unfamiliar coastline. There might be no open beaches in the area he had in mind.

"Three League Beach should be fine," Jens told him. "It's an open beach that stretches for several kilometers. Good sandy bottom that shelves into the land."

"Three League Beach?" Horace asked. "Shouldn't that be closer to fifteen kilometers long?"

Jens smiled. "Mapmakers tend to exaggerate," he said. "I suppose it makes them feel important."

He glanced around the ship and saw that the crew had her ready for departure. With an apologetic gesture, he headed aft for the steering oar, sparing a grin for the figure huddled in his cloak against the port railing.

A few minutes later, they got underway, with the crew rowing strongly against the incoming tide and waves. *Wolftail* slipped out through the breakwater gap and the sailing crew began to hoist the big triangular sail on her starboard side. As the sail filled with a deep *boom*, the ship heeled and started to gather speed. Jens set her on a northeasterly course, sending her plunging and crashing through the waves at a thirty-degree angle to the swell. Spray flew in showers high above the ship, landing on the deck like heavy rain.

Halt groaned miserably and Jens beckoned to the ship's boy, a youngster of fifteen years.

"Yes, skirl?" the boy asked as he walked nimbly down the deck to the stern, swaying easily with the ship's movement.

"Our passenger said he'd be interested in seeing a Skandian helmet, Petter," Jens told him. "Why not show him yours?"

Petter began to turn away, then stopped, recalling a conversation he had overheard among the rest of the crew when Halt had come aboard.

"I've heard that story, skirl," he said. Jens grinned at him and they both looked as Halt lurched to his feet, leaned far over the rail and seemed to call plaintively for someone named Albert.

"Perhaps you could get him a bucket then," he said. "And tell him he'll be better doing that over the lee rail, not the upwind one."

The voyage was a fast one, with no time for Halt to become accustomed to the ship's lurching and heaving. He sat in misery on the deck by the rail, having frequent recourse to the bucket between his knees. Around midday the following day, the ship's motion eased as Jens brought her into the lee of a headland that defined the southern end of Three League Beach.

Jens cast an interrogative glance at Horace. "How's this?" he said. "We're probably ten kilometers to the north of La Lumiere."

Horace studied the deserted coastline. "Looks good to me. Thanks for the ride."

They lowered the sail and rowed *Wolftail* in to shore, her prow grating in the sand as she ran up onto the beach. Coming to a stop, she heeled gently to port. The derrick was rigged once more and the horses were unloaded into the knee-deep water.

Horace took a map from inside his jerkin and unfolded it, studying it and placing a finger on a spot approximating their landing point. He found Chateau des Falaises on the map and estimated that they were approximately two days' ride from it.

"Thanks, Jens," he said. They waited as Halt swung himself over the side of the ship and made his way up the wet sand to where they were standing.

"Did you want us to pick you up when you've done whatever it is you're doing?" Jens asked.

But Horace shook his head. "I'm not sure how long we'll be here," he said. Then, as Halt joined them, he smiled at the Ranger. "You're looking better."

Halt snorted. "Of course I am. The world has stopped pitching up and down like a mad thing." He looked at Jens. "Thanks for the bucket."

Jens grinned. "I'll treasure it as a memento of the man who saved Skandia from the Temujai," he said.

"Mount up, Halt," Horace said, setting his foot in Stamper's stirrup and swinging easily up into the saddle. "We've got to get to Falaise and find somewhere to stay."

They rode at a steady canter, stopping for the night in a small village. Now that they were in Gallica, they assumed the identities they had decided on earlier. Horace became a Teutlandic knight following the tournament circuit, and Halt became his servant, dealing with the innkeeper in the village where they stayed, while Horace remained aloof and haughty, barely deigning to speak. Halt's hair and beard were already overdue for his usual short trim but he let them grow, forming an unruly white mass.

When they reached Falaise, after a day and a half's steady riding, Halt negotiated for the rental of an unoccupied house in a side lane off the main street.

"Best if we stay out of sight," he said, and Horace agreed. "I'll wait a few days then I'll make my way into the castle and look around," the Ranger continued. "That way, the guards will become used to me."

"Now all we have to do," Horace said, "is wait for Maddie and Will to get here."

12

WILL AND MADDIE HAD ASSUMED THAT THE BARON WOULD leave them for several days before he talked with them again. Consequently, they were surprised when they were summoned to meet with him the following day, late in the morning.

"There he goes again," Maddie said, when Will commented on the fact. "He's changing things up, hoping to put us off balance."

"He does like to mess with us, doesn't he?" Will agreed. "Let's see if we can throw him off instead. I'd like to raise a few doubts in his mind about what might be waiting for him if he launches an attack on Araluen."

"You think he's considering that?" she asked.

He nodded grimly. "I'm sure he is."

As ever, Ramon escorted them to the meeting, along with his three armed companions. This time, they met in Lassigny's office at the head of the stairs on the second floor. Armand was present once again, although there was no sign of the Baroness.

Lassigny waved them to seats opposite where he sat behind his desk in his high-backed chair. Armand was beside them, a few meters away, with his chair turned so he could study them.

Ramon and his fellow guards took their positions back from the desk, against the wall.

The Baron treated his two prisoners to another of those long, unblinking stares, his eyes boring into them as they waited for him to speak. By now, they recognized this as another of his gambits, designed to unsettle them and make them nervous. This prolonged silence was designed to put pressure on them, with the possibility that it would cause them to blurt out an inadvertent admission or reveal a fact they would rather keep hidden. Will, however, had decided to break the pattern and take the initiative in the conversation.

"I'm afraid we haven't been completely truthful with you, my lord," he said, breaking the silence. He was watching Lassigny closely and saw the almost imperceptible flicker of surprise in the dark eyes as he caught the Baron off guard.

"Really?" said the Baron, recovering quickly. "And how might that be?"

Will smiled diffidently, maintaining the pretense that this was a friendly discussion between equals. "You asked us about the Araluen Rangers and I feel we may have misled you."

Lassigny shot a sidelong glance at Armand. Then he faced Will and Maddie once more. "In what way?" he asked. He addressed the question to Will but it was Maddie who answered. It was a prearranged plan. The previous night they had discussed their tactics for the next meeting, whenever it might be.

He likes to keep us off balance by constantly switching the subject, Will had said. *So we'll ring our own changes by alternating who answers his questions.*

It was only a small thing but it allowed them to seize the agenda and take control of the conversation.

"As you suspected," she said, "the Rangers are a lot more than simple foresters. They're highly trained, skilled warriors."

Lassigny opened his mouth to question her further, but Will gave him no time to do so.

"They're an elite Corps," he said. "They answer to the King and gather intelligence about the actions of potential enemies. In times of war, they'll scout for the armies and even command some of Duncan's forces when they go into battle."

"They're trained in the art of camouflage and deception," Maddie now added, and Lassigny's eyes snapped back to her. "And they're all expert archers—as you may have gathered already."

Lassigny's eyebrows shot up. "Really? Why would I have thought that?"

Maddie shrugged and pointed toward their weapon case that still stood behind his chair, leaning against the wall. "You've seen our weapons," she said.

"*Your* weapons?" he replied, with a note of scorn in his voice. "What do your weapons have to do with these Rangers?"

"We're both members of the Corps," Will said. "I'm a senior Ranger and Maddie is my apprentice—not my daughter."

The conversation was interrupted by Armand, who gave vent to a short, scornful bark of laughter. The others turned their eyes to him and he made a contemptuous gesture toward Will.

"I might believe that you are one of these so-called secret warriors," he said, "despite the fact that you're an undersized runt. But the girl?" He laughed again.

Will smiled pleasantly in reply. But the smile never reached his eyes. Armand was an arrogant fool, he thought, dismissing

Will because he was shorter than average and seemed to be slightly built. He didn't perceive Will's solidly muscled upper body and arms, the result of years spent drawing an eighty-pound longbow.

"What about her?" he asked mildly. He was pleased to note, after a quick glance at Maddie, that she was unfazed by the Gallican's scorn. She maintained a neutral expression and there was no sign of anger on her face.

Armand leaned forward toward them, speaking slowly and deliberately, as if talking to someone of reduced intelligence. "She's a female. A woman," he said. "Barely more than a *girl!*" He gave the word a contemptuous emphasis. "And women aren't warriors. That's a known fact."

"You might be surprised," Will said. "I've been training her for nearly four years and she's highly accomplished."

"At needlework, perhaps," Armand scoffed. "But at fighting? I think not."

"I could beat you," Maddie said calmly. For a few moments, the room went silent. Then Will reacted quickly.

"No!" he cried. "Maddie, you're not—"

But Lassigny overrode him, waving him to silence. "Just a moment. Is the young lady challenging Armand to an encounter?"

"No, she's not!" Will said, half rising. Behind him, Ramon took a step forward, his hand dropping to the hilt of his sword. Will sensed the movement and sat back in his chair.

Again, Lassigny raised a hand to silence him and turned his smile on Maddie. "Well, young lady? Are you challenging Armand? He is a knight, after all—and a very skillful one."

She glanced dismissively at Armand. "I could beat him," she said.

"Maddie—" Will began, but she met his gaze and smiled calmly.

"It would only be a practice bout, after all." She looked back to Lassigny. "If that would satisfy you, Baron?"

"So you *are* challenging Armand?" he said.

She nodded. "If you permit me to, Baron."

Armand snorted derisively. "Surely, my lord, you can't entertain this idea? It's ridiculous!"

"I agree," Will said quickly.

And now Lassigny turned that sardonic smile on him. "But I don't," he said. "It might be enlightening—and entertaining—to see such a bout." He inclined his head to Maddie. "A practice bout, as you say, with practice weapons."

"Exactly. After all, I have no wish to kill him," she said.

Armand erupted once more. "You? Kill me? You ridiculous, arrogant . . . *girl!*" His rage and indignation got the better of him and he was lost for words.

Maddie continued in that same maddening, unflustered tone. "I propose we fight on horseback, with blunted practice weapons. The first one to unseat the other is declared the winner."

Will opened his mouth to protest once more, then realized that there was no point in doing so. He could tell that Lassigny was going to approve the bout and nothing he could say would stop it.

"So you would use—" Lassigny began, and she finished the statement for him.

"My bow and my saxe. And your knight could use lance, shield and sword."

"That hardly seems like a fair contest," the Baron said.

Maddie chose to misunderstand him. "I know, but I'll try not to hurt him too badly," she said.

By now, Armand was almost apoplectic with rage. "How dare you! You impertinent fool! You arrogant, stupid girl!" He turned his flushed and angry face to the Baron. "Very well, my lord. I'll fight her. And I'll beat her to a pulp! I'll crush her! I will *destroy* her, practice weapons or no."

Will shook his head sadly. "Maddie, what are you doing?" he said. He had no idea that his attempt to unsettle the Baron would end this way, with Maddie's life in danger. Even with a blunted lance, an experienced knight like Armand could easily kill her. Fully armored knights were killed or maimed relatively often in so-called friendly tournaments, and Maddie would have no armor to protect her.

"Don't worry, Will," she replied with a smile. "I know what I'm doing."

Lassigny looked at the two of them, then at his furious henchman. He nodded his head thoughtfully, several times.

"I'll need some time to practice," Maddie said. "And I'll need access to my weapons."

"You'll have them," Lassigny said. "We'll arrange the bout for a week from now. We can make a carnival day of it, so the whole castle and village can watch. As I said, it could be enlightening. And very entertaining."

13

WILL MAINTAINED A TIGHT-LIPPED SILENCE AS THEY STRODE back across the courtyard and up the stairs to their suite of rooms. But once the door was closed and locked behind them, he turned on Maddie furiously.

"Have you lost your mind?" he demanded, and before she could answer, he continued. "Who told you to challenge Armand to a duel? He's a trained knight! He could kill you!"

"It's a practice bout," she pointed out mildly, and he exploded with anger once more.

"A practice bout where he's armed with a lance," he shouted. "You've seen plenty of tournaments. You know that even a practice lance can be deadly!"

"If he manages to hit me," Maddie said. "The lance is a clumsy weapon, and I've got speed and agility on my side. Bumper can run rings around a big, clumsy battlehorse." She paused. "As a matter of fact, that's what I plan to do."

"You've got to do more than run rings around him!" Will told her. "You've got to knock him off his horse! Do you plan to do that with a blunted arrow?"

"No. But I know how I can do it. I spent most of last night

thinking about this, Will. You said you wanted to plant a doubt in Lassigny's mind. Well, what will he think if one of his senior knights is defeated by a girl? That's got to worry him."

"And then what happens to us?" Will demanded. "He'll stop trying to recruit us if he realizes we're a danger to him."

Maddie smiled. "So you admit I've got a good chance of beating Armand?"

He shook his head like a bewildered bull. "I'm not saying you can't. I'm saying this is a very dangerous course of action. Armand could kill you. And if he does, your mother will kill me."

"Or, if I win, Lassigny might think twice about attacking Araluen. Face it, Will, we'll be no worse off. Lassigny was never going to recruit us in any case. And even if we pretended to go along with him, we'd be watched like hawks. It would take us months to win his trust."

Will subsided onto one of the chairs by the table and rested his head in his hands. He realized Maddie was right: As long as there was a chance that Lassigny could recruit them, they would be constantly under surveillance. Finally, he looked up.

"Do you really have a plan to beat him?" he asked. He knew Maddie was no fool. And he knew she was a highly capable warrior.

Maddie smiled. "Of course I do. I wouldn't have started all this if I didn't. I've got several things going for me. For a start, he's arrogant and conceited. And he'll certainly underestimate me. The worst he might expect is an arrow in the face, so I assume he'll wear a full-face jousting helmet."

"That's a pretty safe bet," Will admitted. But he was still puzzled as to how she planned to defeat an armored knight when she was armed with nothing more than blunt arrows and a wooden copy of a saxe.

"I'm glad you think so, because I'm relying on it. On top of that, as I said, I'll have speed and mobility on my side."

"And he'll have strength, power and a four-meter lance on his," Will said. "So how do you propose to beat him?"

Maddie smiled, relieved that Will seemed to have accepted the inevitable and was taking a positive attitude. She pulled out the second chair, sat opposite him and leaned forward, her elbows on the table.

"Here's what I've got in mind," she said.

Word of the proposed duel flashed around the castle like a bout of summer lightning. A surprising number of people were supportive of Maddie, although few of them gave her any real chance of defeating Armand—or even surviving the bout.

Armand was unpopular among the servants, cleaners, waiters and other working staff in Chateau des Falaises. He was arrogant and short-tempered, and inclined to belittle and disparage any of the workers who made a mistake serving him or were slow in doing his bidding. He also wasn't above physical punishment for those who attracted his anger. He was free with his fists when it came to the male servants, and had been known to lash out at some of the female staff with the short riding whip he always carried.

Even the soldiers of the castle garrison disliked him, although they didn't advertise the fact. They were subject to military discipline, after all, and Armand was a senior officer. Any sign they wished him ill or hoped for Maddie to be triumphant could be met with severe punishment.

But on the occasions when Maddie and Will were allowed to exercise in the courtyard, she was aware of a covert attitude of approval and even admiration from Ramon and his three cohorts.

Halt had resumed his daily visits to the castle and overheard several of the staff discussing the contest. He was horrified and, having learned more—although many of the details and descriptions of the proposed event were wildly exaggerated—he took the news to an equally distraught Horace.

"A duel?" Horace said, his voice rising in pitch and volume. "Against an armored knight? She'll be killed!"

Halt looked doubtful. "It's with practice weapons only," he said.

Horace shook his head dismissively. "Nevertheless. She'll be in grave danger. What the blazes is Will thinking?"

"It may not have been Will's idea," Halt warned him. "You know what Maddie's like. She has a mind of her own."

"Well, she's lost her mind with this!" Horace said vehemently. He paced the room for several seconds, then came to a decision. "Nothing for it. You'll have to make contact with them now and get them out."

Halt shook his head. "I can try," he said. "But it'll be tricky. They'll be watched more than ever now this is in the wind. Lassigny's not going to chance that they'll escape and she'll manage to wriggle out of the fight."

His prediction proved to be true. Maddie and Will were kept under close observation as the week progressed. Whereas formerly Lassigny had been content to keep them simply locked in their tower room, now there were guards stationed permanently in the corridor outside.

"After all," the Baron said sarcastically when he visited their rooms to check on the sentries, "we can't have you changing your mind and deciding to leave us. The people would be so disappointed."

For their part, Will and Maddie spent several evenings constructing the blunted arrows she planned to use. Lassigny had her quiver brought to her and they removed the iron broadheads, replacing them with carved hardwood knobs, weighted with lead to match the weight and balance of the originals. Ramon and the guards kept a close eye on them, ensuring that all the broadheads were accounted for and removed from their room each evening.

Maddie grinned as she handed over a needle-sharp bodkin head—the type used to penetrate armor and chain mail with deadly effect.

"I couldn't keep just one of these, could I?" she teased Ramon.

The guard looked around to make sure nobody else was in earshot. "If it was up to me, yes," he said. "But the Baron has noted down how many arrows were in the quiver and what sort of warheads they all had. If I don't return all of them to him, he'll have the skin off my back."

Initially, Lassigny announced that he was going to cancel their daily exercise sessions in the courtyard as well. But Will remonstrated with him, pointing out that Maddie needed to practice shooting with the blunted arrows. They would be lighter than normal arrows and their flight would be different as a result. In addition, she would need access to Bumper, her horse, as she would have to practice shooting from horseback.

After some discussion, Lassigny conceded both points and their exercise time was restored—although their guard was doubled.

A space was cleared in the lawn area behind the keep and Maddie set up a target there—a wooden platter mounted on a tall pole that approximated the size and height of Armand's head when mounted on a battlehorse. Bumper was saddled and brought to her and the two of them had an enthusiastic reunion. Will watched as she mounted and trotted away from the target, turning her horse when she was forty meters away and setting him to a gallop.

Bumper, like all of his breed, accelerated with incredible speed from a standing start, hurtling toward the pole with its circular target at the top. At that speed and distance, Maddie had time to release two arrows in rapid succession, both of them cracking solidly against the platter. On her eighth passage with the target, the wooden platter split lengthwise from the repeated blows and had to be replaced. Maddie had the replacement reinforced with a pewter platter behind it.

She didn't practice any moves or maneuvers with Bumper. She didn't want to give any of her tactics away to observers. She knew Armand had people watching her and reporting back to him. She simply galloped him straight at the target and concentrated on rapid reloading and shooting. But she and Bumper were a long-established team and she knew that, when the time came, he would respond instantly to the directions she would give him with pressure from her knees and legs.

The people who regularly walked and exercised in the garden watched with interest too. They could see her amazing skill and unerring accuracy and they were impressed. But nobody could see how her blunt arrows, no matter how accurately placed, could possibly unhorse a knight of Armand's skill.

And there was no doubt that he was skillful—very skillful.

He began to practice as well, having a quintain set up in the same area. This was a practice target for horsemen armed with a lance. It was a crude effigy of a warrior, hinged and counterweighted and mounted on a pole. It was designed to swivel if it was hit even slightly off center. A weighted sandbag hung from its outstretched arm. If the figure swiveled, the sandbag would whip around and thud painfully into the attacking horseman's back or head.

If the lance struck directly in the center, the quintain would rock backward on its hinge against the counterweight, but the swinging arm would remain still.

Ominously, all of Armand's strikes were dead center. His practice sessions were obviously intended to unnerve his opponent.

"He's good," Will told Maddie, after they had spent several minutes watching the knight practice.

Maddie shrugged. "The quintain isn't ducking," she said, "and it isn't shooting back."

As Lassigny had said, the day of the contest had been declared a carnival day. A large, level field across the causeway bridge, set between the castle and the village, was being prepared for the bout. The long grass was mowed, and on one long side of the rectangular field a covered viewing platform was built for the Baron and his senior staff. Across the field, open bleachers would provide seating for the lower-ranking observers—the villagers and castle workers. Behind the bleachers, food stalls were set up, where the audience could buy pies, fruits and sweetmeats and roasted mutton and pork on skewers.

The higher-ranked viewers on the opposite side would be served their food by the castle's kitchen staff.

Several firepits were dug and prepared, with spits over them where whole sides of pork and beef could be roasted. Fire tubs were put in place and their fire boxes filled with charcoal to boil or roast vegetables.

At the ends of the field, two marquees were provided where the combatants could prepare and, in Armand's case, don their armor. Will and Maddie were permitted out of the castle to inspect the field, under strict guard, of course. Will paced the short cut grass carefully, checking for irregularities, rabbit holes, dips or anything else that might trip Maddie's horse. The sound of hammering and the smell of fresh sawn wood filled the air.

Maddie simply stood in the center of the field, taking in the overall atmosphere, and making note of the position of the sun and its estimated path as the day went on. She noted that on the first passage of arms—the most dangerous one—the sun would be in her eyes. She shrugged. Naturally, the Baron would want to give his man any advantage that he could, but there was nothing she could do about it so she chose to ignore it.

Will joined her after he finished his inspection. "Looks like everyone's in for a lovely day," he said.

She smiled at him. "Everyone except Armand."

14

ON THE DAY OF THE CONTEST, HALT AND HORACE JOINED an excited throng of villagers heading for the jousting field. Horace's insignia of a black bear proclaimed him to be a Teutlandic knight. He wore a long cloak with a deep cowl, which he pulled up to conceal his face. His sword hung on his left side, counterbalanced by a heavy-bladed dagger on the right.

Knowing that Maddie had noticed him several times in the castle grounds, Halt had replaced his blue-and-white-striped cloak with a plain olive-green one, also with the cowl up. He was armed with a saxe under the cloak, and a throwing knife in his boot. In addition, he carried his ever-present staff. He glanced sidelong at Horace, noting the sword in its scabbard.

"Planning on using that?" he asked lightly.

Horace scowled at him. For some reason, he tended to blame the Ranger for Maddie's involvement in this fight—possibly because Halt had been the one to bring him the news.

"If he hurts Maddie, he's a dead man," he said grimly.

"Maddie can look after herself," Halt told him.

Horace merely grunted, and Halt hoped that he was right. They found seats on the second row of bleachers, shoving through to take a central position. Those around them cast resentful looks their way as they moved to make room for them, but said nothing. The bigger man looked bad tempered and not one to trifle with. And besides, he was a knight, even if a foreign one, and the villagers were accustomed to letting knights have their own way.

They had been sitting for some ten minutes when there was a stir in the crowd. Most of the seats were occupied by now and the occupants were all looking to their left. Halt and Horace followed the direction of their eyes and saw Lassigny, his wife and their entourage of knights and ladies entering the field and making their way to their more salubrious seating. It was the first time the two Araluens had set eyes on the Gallican noble.

"Looks normal enough," Halt said. "I expected horns and a tail."

The Baron waved a languid hand to the crowd and received an apathetic round of applause and a few desultory cheers.

"Doesn't seem worried by the lack of enthusiasm," Horace said quietly.

"He's probably used to it," Halt replied.

Once the Baron and his party were seated, the crowd settled down, waiting expectantly for the main players in the day's entertainment. The smell of charcoal smoke and roasting meat wafted across the stands. Horace's stomach rumbled loudly. Even the tension he was feeling couldn't allay his appetite. He considered walking to the back of the stands for some roast pork on a stick, then decided against it. His stomach rumbled again.

"Shut up," Halt told him.

"Don't tell me. Tell my stomach," Horace replied.

There was a buzz of movement in the crowd around them

once more and they heard the drumming of heavy hoofbeats. Then Armand cantered into view, coming from their left and riding along the front of the bleachers, then swinging across the field to salute the Baron.

He was fully armed, in chain mail under a red surcoat that bore his insignia—a depiction of a stooping red hawk—inside a white circle. The same device was emblazoned on his kite-shaped shield and his lance was decorated in spiraling red and white stripes. He wore a full-face jousting helmet, with no visor, merely slits cut in the front for ventilation and vision. His view inside that, Horace knew, would be severely restricted. But his face and head would be well protected.

Horace suddenly seized Halt's arm. "He's wearing a sword!" he said in a fierce whisper. "I thought you said they stipulated practice weapons?"

Halt's eyes narrowed as he peered more closely at the mounted knight. Horace was correct. The sword hanging from his side was no wooden drill sword.

"They did," he replied. "I hope Will's got his eyes open."

Armand had reined in his battlehorse in front of Lassigny's enclosure. The big roan stamped its feet nervously and moved a few paces from side to side. Armand dragged savagely on the reins to curb it. The roan tossed its head, objecting to the heavy-handed treatment. In reply, Armand leaned forward and backhanded it across the head. A murmur of disapproval went through the crowd, but the horse quieted.

"Nice fellow," Halt muttered.

Horace said nothing, but glared at the Gallic knight's back. His hand dropped to the hilt of his sword.

Halt noticed the movement. "Take it easy," he said.

Several minutes passed, then they heard the sound of more hoofbeats—lighter this time than the heavy drumming of a battlehorse's hooves. People stood and craned to see the new-comer.

Maddie cantered into view, coming from their right and sit-ting lightly to Bumper's easy canter. She wore no armor, just a green woolen jerkin over brown tights, with soft leather boots that came halfway up her calves. Her recurve bow was slung over her shoulder and a quiver of arrows hung from her belt. She wore a hat with a long peak and Halt, glancing quickly to check the direction of the sun, understood why.

As Armand had done, she rode along in front of the bleach-ers. She was greeted by a muted growl of approval—none of those present wanted to be too obvious about the fact that they were hoping she'd win. As she passed, Halt and Horace lowered their gazes, so that their faces were concealed in the shadow of their cowls.

Reaching the center of the spectator stands, she wheeled Bumper and rode across the field to stop in front of Lassigny, next to Armand and his battlehorse. The roan danced a few nervous steps as Bumper halted beside him. Again, Armand hauled viciously on the reins to quiet his mount. Maddie glanced contemptuously at him as he did.

Lassigny rose from his seat and stepped forward to lean on the rail at the front of his dais, inspecting the two contestants, looking from one to the other. In no way did this appear to be an even match. Maddie and Bumper were dwarfed by Armand and his massive battlehorse. Maddie appeared to be virtually un-armed, by dint of the fact that her bow was still slung across one shoulder. Armand had couched his lance in the rest built into his right stirrup. The red-and-white-striped weapon appeared huge in contrast to the delicate curves of Maddie's bow, and it towered high above them.

Lassigny smiled sardonically. He fully expected the girl to be smashed into submission. It was more than likely she would be killed. He allowed himself a mental shrug. It would serve her right, he thought, for being so foolish as to challenge Armand with her limited weapons. And it would put her insolent companion well and truly in his place as well. Lassigny still resented Will's having infiltrated his castle so easily, and very nearly managing to escape with Philippe's son, Giles. If it weren't for the informer who had alerted the Baron to the rescue bid, the escape might well have been successful.

He realized that the crowd had fallen silent and the two combatants were watching him curiously, wondering why he was delaying. Let them wonder, he thought, and purposely waited another twenty seconds, staring from one to the other, before he spoke.

"Are you both ready for the contest?" he asked finally.

"Yes, my lord," Armand replied in a booming voice.

"Yes," Maddie said. Her voice was lighter and softer than the heavyset knight's.

"And you have your chosen weapons?" he asked.

This time Maddie was first to answer. "Just what we carry," she said.

Armand glanced at her in annoyance. He considered himself the senior of the two of them and it was his prerogative to speak first. Now he hastened to answer. "Yes, my lord. Lance and sword."

"Then go to your pavilions for any final preparations you

may need. And be ready to answer the trumpet that will call you to battle." He indicated the liveried trumpeter standing at the base of the viewing platform, a burnished silver instrument held under one arm.

The two riders began to turn their horses toward their respective ends of the field when a voice interrupted the proceedings, shouting from Maddie's end.

"Wait! My lord! Wait!"

The crowd's eyes turned as one in that direction. They began to rise to see better, the front ranks first, then the higher levels as they sought to see over their neighbors. A figure was running out onto the field, toward the Baron's stand. A rumble of conversation rolled around the field as people recognized him.

"It's Will!" Halt said, and Horace nodded.

On the dais, Lassigny held up a hand to stop the two riders and they reined back their horses. Again, the roan skittered, stumbling a pace or two, and suffered another savage jerk on the reins, pulling his head sideways and bringing him to a stop. Maddie shook her head at Armand's cruel behavior. The battlehorse was obviously young and nervous.

"My lord, I protest!" Will said as he reached the viewing stand. He was within easy speaking distance now but continued to speak loudly. He wanted the assembled crowd to hear him.

"You protest?" Lassigny said, a sneer on his face and in his voice. "It's a little late in the day for that. If you want to call off the fight, you're too late."

The crowd voiced their agreement. Whether or not they felt any empathy for Maddie, they were here for entertainment—to watch a combat—and they had no wish for that to be curtailed.

"I'm not trying to call it off, my lord," Will said.

Lassigny noted with some satisfaction that the Araluen was now using his proper title. He hadn't done so in any of their previous encounters and it told the Baron that Will was desperate.

"Then what are you . . . protesting . . . about?" Lassigny's tone was dismissive and sarcastic. It left no doubt in anyone's mind that he regarded Will and his protest with complete contempt.

In reply, Will pointed to Armand. "He's wearing a sword," he said. "They were to fight with drill weapons. Wooden weapons."

In the stands opposite, Horace heaved a sigh of relief. "Thank god," he said quietly. Halt grunted agreement. But they spoke too soon.

Lassigny eyed Will for several long seconds, and the smile on his face grew wider. "Your girl stipulated 'blunted weapons,'" he said. "That sword is blunted."

He gestured and Armand drew his sword. To those nearby it was obvious that the edges had been blunted and the point rounded off. A few of those around the Baron called out in confirmation. The people in the bleachers fell silent.

"It's a steel sword!" Will cried. "Blunted or not, it's still lethal. If he hits her with that, he'll—"

He got no further as Lassigny shouted over him. "It's what the girl agreed to!" he roared. "So she'd better take care that Armand *doesn't* hit her!"

Those seated around him voiced their approval. Even a few voices from the public stands were raised. There were some who had placed wagers against Maddie, although the odds they had been offered were highly unattractive. Nobody believed that Maddie could win. Most wagers were based on how many passes she would survive before Armand's lance caught her.

"Get on with it!" someone shouted.

Lassigny leaned forward over the railing in front of him and beckoned Will closer. He lowered his voice to a normal speaking level.

"It's too late to object now, jongleur," he said. "You should have made sure of the conditions when they were being set. The girl agreed to these terms. You can't change them now."

"But—"

Lassigny cut off Will's last attempt with an imperious wave of his hand, raising his voice again so he could be heard all round the arena. "The protest is dismissed! The contest will proceed! Riders, go to your pavilions!"

Maddie and Armand wheeled their horses away, heading for opposite ends of the field. The crowd began to cheer, various groups calling out for their chosen contestant. As the noise level grew, Will remained where he was, glaring at the contemptuous figure above him.

"If anything happens to her," he said softly, so only he could hear, "I'll kill you, Lassigny."

Then he turned on his heel and strode off toward Maddie's pavilion.

15

Bumper was standing patiently outside the pavilion when Will arrived. The little horse neighed a greeting and butted his head gently against Will's shoulder as the Ranger stopped to rub his nose. Inside the tent, Maddie heard her horse's reaction and realized Will was outside.

"Come in, Will," she called. Her voice was pitched a little higher than normal, evidence of the strain she was feeling about the upcoming combat. That was to be expected, Will thought as he pushed the canvas flap aside and entered.

The pavilion was sparsely furnished, with a table and two chairs and a rack to hold armor and weapons. Maddie's bow and quiver were hanging on it. She was seated at the table, breathing steadily, staring straight ahead. A jug of wine and another of water were on the table, along with two beakers.

Maddie looked up at Will. "Just getting myself ready," she told him.

He stopped just inside the door, understanding her preoccupation. He had felt the same way many times, before an imminent combat. She would be settling her nerves, going over her tactics for the fight with Armand, reviewing her ideas and making sure there was nothing she hadn't allowed for. He didn't want to interrupt her or break her concentration.

But she smiled at him—albeit a weak smile. "Don't just stand there. Feel free to talk," she said.

He moved to the table and sat in the chair opposite her. She had poured herself a beaker of water and she raised it to her lips and took a sip.

"Mouth's dry," she explained, setting the beaker down again.

"Understandable," he said. "Anything I can do for you?"

She shook her head. "Just keep me company," she replied.

Will gestured to the untouched wine jug on the table. "I imagine Armand isn't drinking water at the moment."

She smiled again. "Let's hope he's hitting the wine hard."

"His horse is young. Not very experienced," he said.

"I noticed. I hadn't relied on that but it'll be in my favor. I don't like the way Armand treats him," she added as an afterthought.

"I should think the horse doesn't, either. And that'll work for you too. It'll make him more nervous and skittish. A knight and his battlehorse need a good bond if they're going to work well together. Someone like Armand doesn't understand that, of course. To him a horse is just an object—not a living, breathing creature."

"Dad always says your horse is your partner in a battle," Maddie observed.

"He's right. And you know that from the way you and Bumper work together."

It was unimportant, inconsequential talk, but it served to calm Maddie's nerves and steady her breathing and concentration. Will rose and took her quiver from the stand, checking that the arrows were free to move and the shafts weren't crossed over each other. The bow was already strung and he examined the string for any sign of fraying or loss of tension. He knew Maddie would already have done these things, but it didn't hurt to double-check. The nocking point, a small leather disk fastened on the string, marking the correct spot to nock the arrow, seemed to be properly positioned. To make sure, he took an arrow from the quiver and nocked it, checking that it sat at right angles to the bow when the nock was just below the leather disk. Nodding to himself, he replaced the arrow in the quiver.

"It's all looking good," he said.

Maddie nodded. As he had assumed, she had checked her equipment already, but there was always the possibility that Will's experienced eye might catch something she had missed.

There was a small leather pouch hanging from the rack as well. Will picked it up, feeling its unexpected weight. As he moved it, the dozen or so round stones inside grated together.

"You've got your sling?" he asked.

She held up her right arm, showing him the leather thong wrapped round her wrist. She glanced at the doorway to the pavilion.

"What's holding them up?" she muttered.

He touched her arm. "I imagine it's Lassigny's sense of the dramatic. Don't let it get to you."

She shook her head irritably. "It's not getting to me. I just wish they'd—"

She started violently as the sound of a trumpet blast came from outside. Will squeezed her arm, but said nothing. She took a deep breath to steady herself and smiled wanly at him.

"Sorry about that," she said.

He shrugged—a little nervousness was a good thing. It avoided any feeling of complacency or overconfidence.

Then Maddie rose and moved to the arming rack. She clipped the quiver to her belt, slung the shot bag across one shoulder and her bow across the other, then turned to face him as she pulled on her gauntlets.

"How do I look?" she said.

He grinned encouragingly at her. "You'll be the belle of the ball."

She replied with a grin of her own, then strode resolutely out through the doorway. Bumper looked up as she emerged and whiffled a greeting. She patted his muzzle, then gathered his reins and swung lightly up into the saddle. She knotted the ends of the reins together—she'd be using both hands on her bow and didn't want the loose ends trailing when she dropped them. Then she touched Bumper lightly with her heel and swung him away to face the combat ground. Will followed the little horse as he trotted toward the fenced-off area. At the far end, they could see Armand in his red armor, astride the big roan. The horse pranced and danced sideways as his rider jabbed him with his spurs, letting out a small neigh of protest.

Will stopped at the waist-high railing that marked the end of the combat ground. The two riders trotted their horses out onto the mown grass, stopping a hundred meters apart, facing each other. Lassigny's enclosure was at the midpoint between them.

The Baron rose from his seat again and moved to the front of his enclosure, his eyes going from one to the other as Maddie and Armand faced each other. Maddie looked up at the sun behind Armand. It was at three-quarter elevation and she tugged the peak of her cap, adjusting it to shield her eyes. Armand was an ominous figure in red and white. His face was hidden behind the jousting helmet, which was enameled in red. He looked somewhat inhuman—like a towering metal statue sitting astride a huge horse.

With some surprise, she realized that, now they had started, the nervousness had left her and the tight knot of tension that had formed in her stomach was gone. She felt calm, relaxed and settled. She knew her own abilities and was confident in them.

"Ready?" Lassigny called.

Maddie unslung her bow and held it ready in her right hand. She raised it above her head. "Ready!" she called.

Armand raised his shield in his turn. "Ready!" he called, his voice muffled inside the helmet.

The Baron turned to the trumpeter below him. "Sound," he ordered quietly.

The trumpeter licked his lips to moisten them, then raised his instrument and blew a single, piercing note.

And the fight was on.

16

As was his custom, Bumper shot forward like an arrow from a bow, hitting maximum speed within a dozen paces. Armand's roan battlehorse, heavier and clumsier, was slower to accelerate, lumbering ponderously to a gallop.

Maddie angled Bumper to her right, so they would pass Armand on his left side, where he held his shield. As he saw the movement, Armand raised his lance to clear his horse's head, and brought it down so it was pointing across the horse's withers and leveled at Maddie.

They drew closer, and Maddie plucked an arrow from her quiver. Dropping the reins onto Bumper's neck, she nocked it to her bowstring. At forty meters' distance, she raised the bow, drew and let fly, aiming at Armand's head. In spite of the fact that he was wearing a helmet, Armand's instinctive reaction was to raise his shield to deflect the arrow, unsighting himself for a few vital seconds.

The moment she saw the shield come up, Maddie guided Bumper with her knees and thighs and swerved him violently to her left, crossing Armand's path so that she was now approaching from his right-hand side. It was a maneuver no big, heavy battlehorse could ever hope to match, so it was completely unexpected by the Gallican knight, who had previously only dueled against riders mounted on battlehorses.

With only twenty meters to go, Armand lowered the shield and cursed as he saw Maddie was no longer on his left. He searched for her desperately, his vision hampered by the helmet's narrow slits, and found her almost upon him and on his right.

Hurriedly, he brought the lance over his horse's head once more and tried to bring it to bear on Maddie.

It was still coming down into position as they crossed. Maddie, her bow in her right hand, caught the lance tip on the back of the bow and flicked it up, deflecting it over her head. The lance slid along the bow with an ugly rasping sound, then slipped free. It was an astounding feat of hand-eye coordination and split-second timing, but it was the sort of thing that Rangers trained for and she had been mentally preparing for the move for the past few days. She had recalled a story of Will performing a similar deflection of an arrow in flight in Nihon-Ja many years ago.

Armand, his weight braced forward and prepared for the shock of impact against Maddie's body, was caught completely by surprise.

There was no impact, no resistance to his lance, and his tensed body lurched forward in his saddle. The swaying lance suddenly became a four-meter hindrance, threatening to pull him farther out of the saddle. In desperation, unable to control it, he let go and dropped it so that it crashed to the ground and bounced with a shuddering thud that sent vibrations along its length. His horse, already confused by their opponent's move, shied away from the bouncing weapon, so that Armand struggled further to retain his seat.

Cursing, Armand reached for his sword and began to draw it, just as two massive hammer blows clanged against the back of his helmet. Maddie, wheeling Bumper around in a half circle, had let fly with two rapid shots, smashing the lead-weighted hardwood arrowheads into the heavy iron helmet.

At a range of a mere thirty meters, the arrows were traveling at full speed when they hit him. The force of the twin impacts was devastating, throwing Armand forward against the high pommel of his saddle.

Just as bad was the noise—the savage *CLANG!* that came with each arrow. It reverberated inside the helmet, throwing Armand's eyes out of focus for a few vital seconds, leaving him disoriented and off balance once more. Suddenly fearful that he might lose his sword as well as his lance, he let the weapon drop back into its scabbard. His horse, sensing Armand's sudden loss of control, slowed to a trot. Armand shook his head to clear his vision and peered desperately through the helmet's eye slits, searching for Maddie.

There she was!

The fleeting, will-o'-the-wisp figure on the speeding little horse was crossing in front of him, riding in a wide circle around him and, as he watched, releasing another of those cursed arrows.

CLANG!

It slammed into his helmet above the vision slits, rocking him back in the saddle and blurring his sight for a few more precious seconds. The impact was like a strong man repeatedly swinging a wooden mallet at the helmet.

When his vision cleared, Maddie was gone. He dragged furiously at the reins to swing his battlehorse after her.

CLANG! CLANG!

Two more thundering blows on his helmet, from behind this time, sent him rocking forward, grabbing for the pommel to stay astride his horse.

The roan was now thoroughly panicked, as its rider swayed off balance in the saddle. It neighed fearfully and stumbled under the weight of its unsteady rider. Armand sawed viciously at the reins but only succeeded in unsettling the horse even further. It faltered and lurched to one side, its head hauled round by the reins.

Unlike Armand, the roan could see the stocky little piebald riding in a giant circle around it. Fighting against its rider's clumsy efforts to bring it under control, the battlehorse curvetted and turned slowly on the spot as it watched Bumper.

Striving to maintain his balance, Armand saw the unfocused image of the little horse and its rider passing across his front. Expecting a further barrage of arrow strikes, he brought his shield up to cover his face.

But, by the time it was up in position, Maddie and Bumper had galloped round to his right side, and once more, she shot with incredible accuracy.

CLANG!

The helmet was now dented in several places—witness to the force of the arrow strikes at such short range. Maddie's bow could hurl one of those arrows for two hundred meters or more. At a closer range of twenty to thirty meters, the speed and force of the arrows was shattering. Armand reeled in his saddle as Maddie gave him no time to recover from the repeated ringing blows to his head.

The roan stumbled clumsily, trying to turn with Bumper,

but unable to match the smaller horse's speed and agility. It was a vicious cycle: As the roan stumbled, he threw Armand off balance, and as the rider swayed awkwardly in the saddle, he added to the horse's clumsiness. Since he had dropped his lance, Armand had not had a moment when he was solidly, firmly seated. And with each passing moment, the problem became worse.

With slight pressure of her knees, Maddie brought Bumper to a halt, level with Armand's left-hand side, watching as he desperately tried to regain his equanimity. The battlehorse pranced awkwardly with its rider's clumsy movement.

"Now's the moment, boy!" Maddie said to Bumper. She swung him to face the big roan, urging him to full speed as she drew and shot, drew and shot again and again.

CLANG! CLANG! CLANG!

Three massive blows slammed against Armand's helmet, deafening him, blurring his sight and hurling him sideways to the right.

Trying to compensate for his off-center weight, the roan stepped to the right as well, just as Bumper, traveling at full speed, slammed into him, shoulder to shoulder.

Bumper was a good deal shorter than the roan, so the force of his shoulder charge hit the bigger horse on a rising angle, shoving him upward and sideways. Armand, feeling the horse stagger beneath him, tried to retain his balance with wildly windmilling arms. He released his grip on the shield, which went flying.

As the roan was pushed farther off balance, Armand's weight was hurled to the right, past the point of no return. He clutched wildly at the pommel, but too late. Gravity and the weight of his armor took control and he toppled sideways off the staggering horse, his feet slipping clear of the stirrups. He crashed to the ground, driving the wind from his lungs and raising a small cloud of dust and grass clippings with the force of the impact.

He lay on his side, winded and gasping for breath. His arms and legs made small, crab-like motions as he tried to rise, then he went back down again, rolling onto his back.

Without Armand's shifting weight to unbalance it, his horse regained its footing and trotted a few meters away, shaking its head and snorting loudly. It wore a vaguely embarrassed look.

Bumper shook his head too, rattling his mane and the reins still looped over his neck in satisfaction. Ranger horses loved showing up big, clumsy, powerful battlehorses, and Bumper was typical of his breed. Maddie leaned forward and patted his neck.

"Good boy!" she told him, and he shook his head again. "Are you all right?" she added, concerned that the force of his charge against the bigger horse might have injured his shoulder. Bumper danced a few steps to reassure her.

The watching crowd, which had been shocked into silence by the one-sided combat, now came to their feet and roared their approval of the slender young woman and her stocky, shaggy little horse.

In the stands, Halt and Horace exchanged delighted looks.

Horace shook his head, in awe of his daughter. "I knew she'd do it," he said, leaning closer to Halt so he could be heard above the cheers of the crowd. "I just didn't know how."

Halt's lips twitched in the tightest of smiles. "When you and Will were apprentices and always arguing, he had planned to do much the same thing to you. I wonder if he told her?" he mused.

Opposite, Lassigny was white faced with fury as Maddie turned Bumper and trotted lightly to stand before him.

"I claim the victory," she said, her voice carrying above the slowly receding roar of the crowd. Two of Armand's attendants had made their way to the fallen knight, helping him rise groggily to his feet. He removed the helmet, shaking his head, relieved to be rid of its weight and constriction. He looked at the dents in the metal and let the helmet slip from his hand and fall to the ground, then walked unsteadily to stand beside Maddie, before Lassigny.

"My lord . . . ," he said shakily. "Pardon, please! I—" He got no further as Lassigny unleashed his rage.

"Get out!" Lassigny screamed, his voice rising to a high-pitched shriek. "Get out of my sight and get out of my castle! You incompetent fool! How dare you stand before me! Go!"

He shot one hand out, with his forefinger pointing to the road that led to the village, away from Chateau des Falaises.

Armand gaped at him, uncomprehending. "My lord?" he queried.

But Lassigny was beside himself, almost incoherent with rage. "Go! Get out of here! You sicken me! Go and never let me see your miserable, incompetent face again!"

Silence fell over the crowd as the defeated knight, his head hung in shame, turned and trudged away from the field of combat. Lassigny paid him no further attention. Color was slowly returning to his face as he turned to Will, who had joined Maddie before him.

"As for you, jongleur," Lassigny said, his voice falling back to a more normal timbre, "you and your companion will pay a heavy price for this. You've deceived me and made a fool of me—and nobody does that." He looked around to where Ramon and his contingent of guards were standing by, regarding Maddie with amazed admiration.

"Take them back to the tower," Lassigny ordered. "They are spies and they will suffer the fate of all spies. A week from today, they will hang."

17

Life in their tower room became considerably less comfortable for Maddie and Will. The tasty and varied meals they had been receiving were replaced with a constant diet of thin barley gruel, bread and cold water. The steaming, fragrant pots of coffee and crusty bread loaves were no more.

In addition, in the evening after the combat, Ramon barged into their room and stripped the two blankets from each of their beds, shrugging as Will questioned him.

"Baron's orders," he said briefly, rolling the four blankets into a bundle and exiting.

"What was that about?" Maddie asked.

"Maybe he thought we might make a rope so we could reach past the plastered areas of the wall outside the window—to a point where we could find hand- and footholds," he said. "At least we still have our cloaks to cover ourselves when we sleep."

"Maybe we could make a rope out of them?" Maddie suggested.

Will shook his head. "Four blankets would provide a lot more material than two cloaks. You'd need to tear them into strips, then plait the strips together to provide strength. The plaiting reduces the length, so you'd need more material. The cloaks would never do it."

Maddie bowed her head apologetically. "I'm sorry, Will. This is all my fault. I shouldn't have challenged Armand."

She was surprised when Will disagreed. "Lassigny was toying with us," he said. "We were never going to work for him, and even if we had planned to, and he decided he wanted us to, it would have taken months to gain his trust. This way we've done what we intended. We put a big doubt in his mind about the idea of attacking Araluen once he has taken the throne."

"Won't do us much good," she said. "After all, he plans to hang us."

Will smiled encouragingly. "We're not dead yet," he said. "We've got six more days to find a way out of here."

But even that was looking more difficult. There were now guards permanently stationed outside their door, so the idea of picking the lock and escaping that way was no longer practicable.

"Why's he doing this?" Maddie asked. "I mean, if he wants to execute us, why not just do it? Why give us a week's grace?"

"He wants us to suffer," Will told her. "He wants us to think about it as we see the day getting closer and closer. I imagine as a boy he enjoyed pulling the wings off flies."

She shook her head. "Never thought I'd see a fly as a kindred spirit," she said morosely.

Will dropped a hand on her shoulder. "Don't worry. We'll think of something," he told her. He had already decided that if the worst came to the worst, he would roll up the cloaks, knot them together and, leaning out the window, lower Maddie to a point past the smoothed-over stonework—from which she could climb down. Of course, that would leave him trapped in the room to face the Baron's wrath, but he had already accepted that possibility, as long as he could set her free.

"Well, I hope you do," she said, "because I'm all out of ideas."

"I'll have to get them out tomorrow night," Halt said.

He was busy winding strips of burlap around his longbow. He had stripped a small sapling, keeping its bark in one piece as far as possible, and wrapped the bark around the bow to disguise its smooth surface, giving it the appearance of a roughly trimmed staff. Then he plastered it liberally with gray river mud to conceal it further. He had unwound the leather grip that was bound around the middle of the bow and stowed it in his pocket. The bowstring, along with two spares, would be inside the hood of his cloak.

"How do you plan to do it?" Horace said. He regarded the bow critically. It certainly didn't look anything like a longbow anymore.

"When the bell rings for the gates to close, I'll sneak into the stables and hide out in the stall with Bumper and Tug. Once it's dark and the castle is asleep, I'll make my way to the keep and up to the roof. Their room faces the keep. But it's a floor higher than the roof. I'll shoot a line to them and they can slide down to me."

Horace regarded the equipment Halt had assembled on the rough table in their small room.

Among the coils of rope and fine twine were two strange items. They were cylinders carved from wood, about the size of a water beaker. One end of each was covered with thin leather, scraped and shaved until it was translucent. It was pulled tight and bound in position with twine, overlaid with melted beeswax. Horace tapped one experimentally. It was taut as a drumskin. The thin leather was pierced in the center, leaving a small hole.

Halt glanced up as he did so. "Careful with that," he warned. "They're a bit delicate for your big, clumsy hands."

"What are they for?" Horace asked, and Halt replied with one of his rare smiles.

"It's something I saw years ago in Toscana," he said. "It was a children's toy and I've been trying to find a practical use for it ever since. And now I have."

The tone of his voice and the sly expression on his face told Horace that he wasn't going to provide further detail. The tall knight shrugged and set the cylinder down again.

"Once you've got Maddie and Will down to the roof of the keep, how do you plan to get out of the castle?" he asked.

"We'll head back to the stables," Halt said, "and wait till the morning. The gates open for day visitors at the seventh hour. I've been watching and Will and Maddie aren't given their breakfast until half an hour after eight. Before anyone notices they're not in the room, I'll arrange a diversion and they can slip out in the confusion."

Horace chewed his lip doubtfully. "That's a lot of sneaking around in the keep tower and the stables," he said. "Do you think you can manage it without being seen?"

Halt gave him a pitying look. "We're Rangers," he said. "It's what we train for."

"How do I look?" Halt asked. He turned around several times so that Horace could inspect him. He had foregone his usual blue-and-white-striped cloak again in favor of the olive-green one. The blue-and-white-striped garment would be a little too visible in the darkness of the coming night.

Underneath the cloak, he had a pack strapped to his back, containing the equipment that he would use that night, along with a canteen of water, some dried meat and fruit, and a flat loaf of bread. A coil of strong rope was slung around his shoulders, concealed by the cloak. His quiver of arrows hung from the back of his belt, where the cloak would cover it as well. His saxe was in his right boot and his throwing knife was concealed in his left. The rough-looking staff was in his right hand.

Horace studied the staff. The clay had hardened overnight, disguising the slender, even shape of the bow stave. He had to admit that it looked like a staff—thick and irregular in shape.

"Did you want me to wait for you tomorrow at the end of the causeway?" Horace asked.

The Ranger vetoed the idea. "You might be a bit obvious," he said. "You're half a head taller than anyone around here. I'll tell Will and Maddie to keep straight on for the village once they're across the causeway. You could wait for them at the end of the high street, then bring them here."

"What about you? You're not coming with them?" Horace asked.

"The guards at the gate know me and they're used to seeing me on my own. I'll join you later, before anyone realizes they're not in the tower."

Faintly, they heard the clang of a bell from the castle. It was repeated four times.

"That's the signal for the gates to open," Halt said. "I'd better be on my way."

He slipped out of the front door of the little house and made his way down the lane to the village high street. Already people were streaming out of houses and shops along the street, laden with goods that they would sell to the castle inhabitants, as they did every day. At the end of the causeway, they were joined by a small procession of carts bringing produce from outlying farms in the area. Halt merged into the steady flow, blending in with the others, allowing the human tide to carry him along as they made their way across the causeway to the lowered drawbridge and the castle gates.

The usual complement of guards was waiting at the gates, checking the incoming stream for anyone or anything out of the ordinary. They checked the contents of the handcarts and horse-drawn carts, prodding and poking under the tarpaulins that covered the contents with the butts of their spears and halberds.

But the searching and inspections were perfunctory, to say the least. It was a task they carried out every day and there was rarely anything that took their notice. Familiarity had bred a certain carelessness—or lack of attention—in their actions.

They waved the carts and people through in a constant stream. One of them recognized Halt, who was now a permanent fixture at the gates each morning.

"Hello there, Tomkin," he said. "Nice new cloak you've got there. And not before time. That old one was more holes than cloak." He grinned.

Halt bobbed his head obsequiously. "Days are getting colder," he said. "Had to buy a new one."

"Where'd you get the money?" the guard asked, absentmindedly checking a handcart filled with firewood kindling before waving it through the gates.

Halt grinned slyly. "I bet on the girl t'other day," he said.

The guard laughed. "Good for you!" he said. "Wish I'd done the same. But who knew how good she was? Shame they're going to hang her," he added in a casual tone that said he didn't care one way or the other. He jerked a thumb in the direction of the inner gateway. "Through you go, old feller," he said.

Halt bobbed his head and shuffled through into the court-yard. He let his gaze run up the solid bulk of the keep tower, flat roofed and heavy in comparison with the graceful corner towers of the castle.

"And now we wait for tonight," he said to himself.

18

HALT SPENT MOST OF THE DAY IN THE GRASSED RECREATION area behind the keep. True to his disguise, he sat slumped against a stone bench, wrapped in his cloak, his begging bowl on the ground before him. From time to time, a passerby would drop a coin or two into his bowl; Halt would nod his head and touch his finger to his brow in thanks.

"Bless you, stranger," he would say in a whiny, singsong old voice. "The gods love a generous giver."

Aside from the occasional donation, nobody took any undue notice of him. Around midday, several of the food stall proprietors brought him small tidbits of food and he thanked them in the same way. By now, he was a regular element in the daily scene and had become virtually invisible—certainly not worthy of notice or comment.

As the afternoon drew on, he rose and moved to a new position at the rear of the keep, near the northeast tower. Late in the day, with the sun gone from the bailey, masked by the towers and the curtain wall, the day visitors started to drift toward the gates again. The stall holders, seeing their trade slow, began packing up their stalls, preparing to leave for the night.

A small stream of day visitors moved down the eastern side of the keep tower, heading for the main gates. Halt joined them, moving slowly and steadily, and angling his way out to the edge of the crowd, close to the castle wall. As before, nobody seemed to take notice of him as he shuffled along, his staff striking the cobblestones of the courtyard floor in a steady rhythm.

The stables were situated on the eastern side of the castle, level with the front wall of the keep tower. Halt glanced around surreptitiously as he approached them. Nobody seemed to be watching him. He slowly moved out of the stream of people and lowered himself to one knee, fiddling with the fastenings of one of his boots. Again, nobody took any notice, nobody called out to ask what he was doing.

A few meters away, on the other side of the small crowd, a day laborer tripped on a broken cobblestone and dropped his bundle of tools—a shovel, a crowbar and several assorted hammers. The tools clattered and clanged as they bounced on the cobblestones. Those nearest the laborer stepped clear hurriedly and the rest of the crowd turned to look in the direction of the noise.

It was a heaven-sent opportunity for Halt. With a quick glance around to check that nobody was looking his way, he rose to his feet and slipped through the big double doors and into the stable, with a mental prayer of thanks that they hadn't been locked.

Once inside, he closed the doors behind him and stood with his back to them, taking stock of his surroundings.

The interior of the stables was dim and smelled of a mixture of hay, horses and fresh dung. There was no sign of the bad-tempered stablemaster. Halt assumed he was on the upper floor, or perhaps he had gone to the keep for a midafternoon snack or drink. Most likely the latter, Halt thought. He had observed the man over the past week and was familiar with his habits.

Around half of the stalls were occupied, he was pleased to note—that boded well for his plans. A dozen heads were thrust over the stall doors, turning his way and watching him with big, brown eyes. Horses were curious beasts, he knew. At the innermost end of the line, he saw two shaggy heads watching him from one stall. Moving silently along the row of watching horses, he made his way to them. Bumper and Tug recognized him and nodded their heads up and down to let him know. Being Ranger horses, they made no sound. They were trained not to.

"Hello, boys," he said quietly, patting their soft noses. Since he had spoken first, they both made subdued rumbling noises of greeting deep in their chests.

Outside, he heard the gate bell sound four times, signaling that it was time for day visitors to leave. The crowd gathering round the gatehouse would be intensifying, he thought, all trying to push through at once and get home to their fireplaces and a hot drink. From previous observation, he knew that the gate guards would pay only cursory attention to the departing visitors. They were more interested in checking people trying to get into the castle grounds than out of them.

He unlatched the door to the stall and stepped inside, moving between the two shaggy bodies to the rear wall. He checked the water and feed bins and saw they had been recently filled. He nodded in satisfaction. That meant he was unlikely to be disturbed by a stable hand, or the stablemaster himself.

He took off his cloak and unslung the pack and his quiver. Then he lifted the coil of rope from around his shoulders and placed it with the rest of his gear against the wall. He leaned his bow, still disguised as a staff, alongside them and redonned his cloak. Then he scuffed some of the straw together with his boot, making a pile at the rear of the stall. He sank down onto it, his back against the wall, pulling his cloak around him and the cowl up over his head so that his face was in shadow. The two horses turned their heads to watch him curiously. He smiled at them.

"Alert," he said softly. It was the command that would ensure they would warn him if anyone approached the stall. Seated as he was, wrapped in his dark green cloak and with the two horses in front of him, he would be well concealed from any casual passerby, but it never hurt to make sure. He sighed, moved a little to make himself comfortable, and closed his eyes.

Might as well sleep while I have the chance, he thought. It's going to be a long night.

The horses woke him several hours later, their low warning nickers bringing him instantly awake. He could hear someone moving in the stables. A glow of light flared briefly, then dimmed to a steady level as a lantern was lit and trimmed. This was repeated several times, providing a low level of illumination to the interior of the stable. He guessed it was usual nighttime routine for the stablemaster. He saw a dim shadow cast onto the stable walls as the man moved between him and the lanterns. Then a door slammed on the other side of the stable and everything was still again.

"Good boys," he told Tug and Bumper. "Settle down."

In the courtyard outside the stable, he could hear faint sounds of people moving and talking and he guessed it was still early in the evening. This was confirmed a few minutes later when he heard the gatehouse bell toll seven times.

"Two hours to go," he muttered. He'd decided to make first contact at nine hours. The castle's inhabitants would still be eating or relaxing in the dining hall after their meal at that time and there would be less chance of encountering anyone on the keep stairs. At the same time, he didn't want to leave it too late. Will and Maddie would need to be awake so that the sound of voices from their room wouldn't alert the sentries outside in the corridor.

He settled back down to wait. Like so many things, the ability to remain still and patient was part of a Ranger's training.

Time passed, with the gatehouse bell marking its slow passage. When he heard it striking nine, he rose and gathered his equipment together, concealing the pack, quiver and coiled rope beneath his cloak. Then, taking the bow in his hand, he patted the two horses again, stepped out of the stall and headed for the big doors that led into the courtyard.

He opened the double doors a meter or so and peered through the narrow gap. He checked to either side, then up to the walkway inside the battlements. There were a few people still moving about in the bailey, and he could see several sentries on the walls. None of them faced into the courtyard. Their job was to watch for danger from the outside.

He slipped out through a narrow gap in the doors, closed them behind him, then walked casually toward the entrance to the keep. There was no need to run or try to avoid being seen. There was nothing suspicious about a person moving in the courtyard at this hour. If he was observed, there was no reason for any alarm to be raised.

Even so, it was difficult to remain looking casual when his nerves were stretched tight as fiddle strings. He made it to the keep door, glanced around, then opened it and went in. He closed the door behind him. The entry hall was unoccupied and he let out a pent-up breath in relief, leaning back against the door for a few seconds.

The dining hall for lower-ranked castle staff was to his left and he could hear the low mumble of conversation coming from there. As he watched, several kitchen hands crossed the entry hall, carrying trays and jugs from the kitchen. Nobody took any notice of him. He waited till they were out of sight, then walked quickly to the staircase, going up the steps, his soft-soled boots making virtually no sound.

On the next floor, he passed the doorway to Lassigny's office and crossed quickly to one of the circular stairways set into the corners of the tower.

Again, nobody saw him and he entered the dimly lit stairway with another breath of relief and continued upward.

He reached the top floor without encountering anyone and glanced around, taking stock of his surroundings. The top floor was an open space, and obviously served as an armory. Weapons, shields and armor were stored along the walls. In the center were long benches, where swords and spearheads could be sharpened and chain mail repaired. Behind the work benches, a wooden ladder staircase went up to a trapdoor that led to the flat roof.

He mounted the ladder and climbed swiftly to the top. There was no lock on the trapdoor, which made sense: The roof was a defensive fighting position and, in the event of an attack, it wouldn't do to be searching for a key to the lock. He pushed it up, holding on to it so it didn't slam down as it came fully open, and climbed out onto the roof.

Carefully, he closed the trapdoor behind him and, crouching low, made his way to the balustrade facing the northwest tower. He looked up to the top row of windows, some eight or nine meters above the roof of the keep. There was one window showing the warm yellow light of a lantern inside. He smiled grimly to himself. Will and Maddie were still awake, he thought.

He slipped off his cloak and began arranging his equipment.

19

WILL AND MADDIE WERE SITTING AT THE TABLE, FACING each other. On the tabletop, Will had sketched a chessboard with a piece of charcoal, and then had fashioned chessmen from small squares of parchment, with the pieces' symbols drawn on them. Cooped up day and night in the tower, with no exercise period, the hours dragged and they had been glad to have something to pass the time. Maddie had learned the game as a child and had taught it to Will, after instructing him in the construction of the board and pieces. Now she was somewhat miffed that he had rapidly overtaken her in the skills of the game. When they played, he usually won.

It seemed that he was about to do so once more. She had lost most of her major pieces and was down to her queen, the king and one castle. Will, on the other hand, had lost a knight and a bishop. The rest of his pieces crowded round hers, threatening her king.

She rested her chin on her hands and peered at the board, looking for a way out of her predicament. Slowly it dawned on her that her queen was pinned by one of Will's castles. If she moved it, she would expose her king, which she wasn't allowed to do. Her only path was to take the castle with her queen. Then, in turn, Will's remaining bishop, guarding the castle, could take her queen—a totally unsatisfying and uneven trade. The queen was far more valuable than the castle.

She let go a deep sigh of frustration. As she did, the heavy gust of her breath picked up the chessmen and scattered them across the table.

Will regarded her quizzically. "I take it you give in?"

She spread her hands in apology. "Sorry. I didn't mean to do that," she said.

He raised one eyebrow, in that maddening movement she had never been able to match—which was possibly why she found it maddening. "Of course not," he said, his voice dripping with disbelief.

"No! Honestly, I—"

THUD!

Something hit the wall outside the window, striking the wooden outer frame and vibrating rapidly. They both came upright, their eyes shooting first to the window, then to the door to see if the guards outside had heard the sound.

There was no reaction from the men in the corridor. Evidently, the heavy door had blocked the sound. Exchanging a glance, the two rose from the table and moved quickly to the window. Maddie unlatched it and eased it open and they both peered out, heads and shoulders through the opening.

A long black arrow was embedded in the wooden window frame. Will frowned, then studied the fletching: two black flights with a white cock feather. His eyebrows shot up in disbelief, then he grinned delightedly.

"That's one of Halt's arrows!" he told Maddie.

She slapped her forehead with the palm of her hand. "Halt!" she said. "Of course! I knew that beggar looked familiar!"

He regarded her curiously. "Beggar? The one you mentioned before?"

Maddie nodded. "He's got long, shaggy white hair and beard and he wears a blue-and-white-striped cloak. I thought he looked familiar!"

"You never mentioned—" he began, but he was interrupted. The arrow jerked several times and they realized there was a thin cord attached to it, leading away and down into the darkness.

Maddie gestured to it. "Better pull that in," she said.

Will took hold of it and began to carefully wind it in. As it came tight, they could see that it led to the roof of the keep tower, forty meters away and slightly below them. A dark figure was just visible at the edge of the roof, behind the meter-high balustrade.

After a few meters, Will felt a more substantial weight on the cord. He kept pulling, taking care not to put too much strain on the line, and eventually recovered a heavier line—a strong rope. Attached to it was a strange wooden cylinder, looking for all the world like a beaker.

Maddie frowned at it. "What's that?"

Will turned a wide grin in her direction as he carefully untied it. "It's something Halt saw years ago, when I was an apprentice," he said. "We messed around with it for days, trying to find some practical use for it. Looks like he's finally found one." He shook his head, laughing quietly.

Maddie shifted her feet, fairly dancing with curiosity. "But what is it?"

Will carefully untied the thin cord, then secured the heavier rope to one of the bed frames. He passed the thin line through a small hole in the cylinder's base, which Maddie could now see was made of tight vellum. He tied a knot in the end of the line to secure it, then raised the cup to his mouth, carefully pulling the line taut.

"Halt?" he said, into the cup. "Is that you?"

Maddie, by now totally intrigued, watched as he plucked the string once and quickly moved the cup to his ear, listening intently. Faintly, she heard the scratchy sound of an answering voice inside the cup. It was too faint for her to make out the words, but Will's grin told her he had been right. He looked at her.

"It's him!" he said triumphantly.

"What *is* that thing?" she demanded in an absolute fit of curiosity.

Will brought the cup to his mouth again and spoke slowly into it. "Halt? Just a moment."

There was a pause, then the string vibrated as it was plucked from the other end. Will turned to her in explanation.

"It's a way of speaking to each other over a distance," he explained. "Halt saw it when he was in Toscana many years ago. It was a children's toy but he thought it might be useful. The string, when it's pulled tight, carries the vibrations of your voice along it. Then the tight vellum in the base absorbs the vibrations and magnifies them so you can hear the other person speaking. It's quite amazing really. When we want to speak, or let the other person speak, we pluck the string to let them know." He did so now and raised the beaker to his mouth again.

"Halt?" he said. "Can you get us out of here?"

He put the cup to his ear and again, Maddie heard the faint

scratching sound of Halt's voice as he passed his instructions. Will listened intently, then nodded, realized that Halt couldn't see him and spoke once more into his cup.

"All right. Got that. Let me know when you're ready."

A few seconds passed, then the line jerked again. Will began to haul it in and felt something sliding up the rope. He explained to Maddie as he brought the line in.

"He's sending up two harnesses so we can slide down the rope. But he says we'll wait until the castle's well and truly asleep. People looking up won't see the rope against the sky, but they might well notice two dark shadows sliding down it."

The end of the cord came through the window, with two short lengths of rope attached. They were half a meter in length, with a loop at either end. Will placed them on the floor and looked at Maddie.

"You've used one of these before, haven't you?"

She nodded. "We trained with them at the Ranger Gathering last year," she said.

Will busied himself refastening the rope around the bed frame into a slipknot, then attaching the lighter line to the end of it. "Good," he said. "Now all we have to do is wait."

At times like this, it seemed to Maddie that most of her life was spent waiting. They snuffed out the lantern and sat in the darkness as the bell in the gatehouse tolled the passing hours. It was past midnight when they saw the rope jerking again. Will crossed quickly to the window and replied, tugging the rope several times. He gestured for Maddie to check the door and she crossed the room silently, putting her ear to the heavy wooden planks. After listening for a few seconds, she looked at Will and shook her head. There was no sound from the two sentries outside. They had heard the guard change an hour ago and knew that the current pair would be on duty for three more hours. Until then, the sentries would doze in their chairs outside the door.

Halt and Will had discussed this when they had spoken earlier. It was best that they didn't talk any further. The cups and string required Will to speak quite loudly to create the necessary vibrations and there was a chance that once the castle was settled for the night, the guards might overhear Will talking and open the door to investigate.

He gestured to the window. "You first," he told Maddie. "I'll follow when you're down."

He lifted the rope so that it rested over the top of the window frame, giving Maddie room to fit under it. She eased herself onto the windowsill, her legs hanging over the drop, then, taking the short length of rope, she passed it over the top of the heavier cable, and held the end loops in her hands, crossing it so that she could tighten or release its grip on the longer rope by pulling her hands apart or bringing them closer together. That way, she could control her speed as she slid down the rope, making sure she didn't simply go faster and faster until she slammed into the balustrade wall on the keep.

She tightened her grip on the two loops, looked at Will and saw him move his head in the direction of the keep.

"Get going," he whispered.

She slithered her buttocks off the windowsill and dropped away into the night.

20

She felt a moment of panic as the rope stretched under her weight and she dropped vertically for a meter or so. Then the rope came taut and she stopped falling. She recalled now that when she had practiced with this system at the Gathering, that initial drop had always been the worst part. There was always the fear that the rope would snap and she would continue to plummet vertically down.

Now she was sliding down the rope at an angle, the rope that she held on to making a sizzling sound as it passed over the rough surface of the main rope. Her cloak billowed out behind her and she felt a sense of exhilaration as she accelerated down toward the keep.

Too fast, she thought, and pulled her arms apart, so that the hand rope, looped over the main cable, pulled tighter, slowing her descent. The ropes whirred louder as the friction increased.

Looking down, she saw Halt's dark shape by the balustrade. There was a moving gantry set on the balustrade, designed to support tubs of boiling water or oil. Halt had passed the rope over the top of it so that she would slide in above the meter-high wall, rather than slamming into the face of the keep. She slowed her descent further, tightening the handhold's grip on the cable as she approached the wall. The rope whirred louder as she slowed down.

Halt was standing waiting to help her. She raised her legs to clear the balustrade, then felt his firm grip on her arm and a hand around her shoulders as he brought her to a stop, her feet finding purchase on the roof.

For a few moments, she clung to him, her arms around his neck.

"Oh, Halt, it's so good to see you! How on earth did you get here? How did you know we were in trouble?"

He put a warning finger to his lips and she realized that in the excitement, she had been babbling and her voice had been louder than she had intended. She bobbed her head in apology and he leaned closer to her and whispered.

"Time for explanations in a minute. Let's get Will down first."

She nodded, somewhat chastened, and stood back as he tugged on the rope three times to signal Will that they were ready for him.

In the tower, Will felt the signal. He and Halt had discussed this part of the escape earlier. He untied the rope from the bed frame, then refastened it with a slipknot, tugging with his full weight against it to make sure it was holding firm. Then he took the thin cord that they had used to connect the speaking cups and tied it around the free end of the heavier rope. When it was pulled, the slipknot would release and the rope would fall free. Then they could haul it in from the keep tower so that it wasn't left hanging over the courtyard, showing how they had escaped.

He gathered the twine, making sure there were no tangles or snags in it, and dropped it out the window so that it hung above the courtyard in a long bight. He fastened the upper end to his belt, took the rope handles and sat on the windowsill, wrapping the shorter length around the long rope as Maddie had done.

He took a last look around the room, grinned to himself and muttered, "Good old Halt." Then he slid off the windowsill, dropping vertically for several meters as Maddie had done.

The rope came taut and he started to slide, controlling his rate of descent with the rope handholds. The main rope was greased to help him slide more smoothly, and as the friction increased under his greater weight, the grease actually began to smoke with the heat.

Behind him, the trailing length of twine gradually rose out of the void. When he crossed the balustrade, assisted by Halt, it had formed into a long, loose loop behind him, stretching from the keep wall to the window in the northwest tower.

He staggered a few steps as his feet hit the keep roof. Halt's strong hand steadied him and he regained his balance quickly. Then he embraced his old mentor, slapping him on the back as he did so.

"How did—"

Halt quickly silenced him, saying in a fierce whisper, "Time for that later. Let's get that rope down."

Will nodded and untied the cord from the back of his belt. He pulled on it and felt a momentary resistance. The slip knot was tightly fastened. Gradually, he increased the tension on the cord. After a few moments, he felt it coming loose in his hand as the slipknot far above them finally released. The heavy rope sagged and Halt pulled it in, coiling it over his shoulder as he did.

"Ready?" he asked, and his two companions nodded. "Then follow me."

He gathered his equipment and headed for the trapdoor in the roof, leading the way down to the top floor below. Maddie followed him, with Will bringing up the rear. He closed the trapdoor behind him. An important part of the escape plan was to leave no clues as to how they had managed it. Once they were all down the ladder stairs in the big open armory, Will put his hand on Halt's arm and stopped him.

"Where are we going?" he asked, keeping his voice low.

"The stables," Halt replied in the same lowered tones, and Will felt a moment of relief. He had been afraid that they might have to abandon Tug and Bumper.

Halt continued. "We'll wait until first light, then you can break out. I'll organize a diversion to cover your escape."

He led the way to the spiral staircase in the corner and they began to move down, their soft-soled boots silent on the stone steps. They emerged onto the second floor and Halt gestured toward the wide central staircase, then started toward it. Again, Will stopped him.

"Just a moment," he said. They were outside the door to Lassigny's office, which faced the top of the wide stairway. Halt frowned in irritation at the delay but Will moved quickly to the door and opened the latch. At this time of night, he knew, there would be nobody inside.

The office was in darkness but he remembered the layout and moved quickly past the desk to the wall behind it. As he had hoped, their weapons case was still there, leaning against the stone. He slipped off the leather cap and felt inside. Both bows were there—Maddie's had obviously been replaced after the duel with Armand. He slung the case over his shoulder and went back out the door, where Maddie and Halt were waiting, Halt impatiently.

"Are you quite finished?" he whispered sarcastically. Will motioned for him to lead on.

They padded quietly down the stairs, pausing at the bottom to make sure there was nobody around, then slipped like three shadows across the darkened entry hall to the main door.

It was locked for the night, with a heavy wooden locking bar in place. Will lifted it carefully out of the iron brackets set on either side of the door and leaned it against the wall. There would be no way to replace it once they were outside but, without any indication that they had reached the keep roof, they would have to trust to luck that nobody would connect the unlocked door to their escape.

Halt ushered them out, keeping careful watch on the stairs and the entrance to the large sleeping chamber. They huddled against the outside wall of the keep, staying in the shadows. This late in the night, they couldn't hope to carry off Halt's earlier casual manner. They would have to stay concealed as much as possible. He led them along the wall to the end of the keep building, stopping at the open space across the courtyard that led to the stable door. He pointed to the curtain wall, indicating the walkway where sentries stood guard. They could see several of them dimly silhouetted against the starlight, but as Halt had noticed earlier, they all seemed to be facing outward, looking for potential attackers approaching the chateau.

Halt beckoned them closer as they huddled in the shadows by the keep wall. He pointed to himself, then to Maddie, then Will.

Me first, he mouthed. *Then Maddie, then you.*

They nodded their understanding and, with another quick glance at the battlements, he slipped away from the keep, ghosting across the courtyard to the doors of the stables.

They were unlocked still, as he had left them earlier. He shook his head, grateful for the stablemaster's lazy nature and slack habits. He cracked the doors open and slipped inside, holding one of the doors just open and leaving a small gap through which he could watch Maddie's progress.

At the keep, Maddie was about to step out into the open when Will's hand closed on her shoulder and stopped her. She turned to him, a question on her face, and he pointed toward the northern end of the courtyard.

Two guards were on foot patrol, walking down the open space between the keep and the outer wall. Ostensibly, they should have been checking doorways and windows along their route, but they were talking quietly, engrossed in their conversation. They did this patrol five nights a week and had never seen anything out of the ordinary. Consequently, they didn't expect to see anything and so had become careless.

Will and Maddie, huddled in their cloaks, crouched at the base of the keep wall, in the shadow cast by the gatehouse towers, cowls up and heads bowed. As the two sentries came close, Will and Maddie remained totally still, even shallowing their breathing to reduce movement and sound to the slightest possible. In this sort of situation, they both knew, the safest path was to remain absolutely motionless.

The two sentries passed by, their quiet voices audible to the two crouching Rangers. Then the sentries went round to the right to cross in front of the keep until they were out of sight.

Will put his mouth close to Maddie's ear. "Go now."

She slipped away like a wraith, a dark shape in the dimness of the courtyard. Will waited, seeing the gap in the door open as she passed through, then close behind her. Then, with one final look at the battlements, he followed her.

A minute or so later, the three of them were inside the stable with the doors shut, safe from view. Will let out a sigh of relief, then turned to Halt.

"All right," he said. "Let's have it. What in blazes are you doing here? How did you find out we were in trouble?"

"It was Duncan's idea," Halt explained. "He didn't really trust Philippe. He suspected that if something went wrong, Philippe would leave you twisting in the wind. So he sent us along as backup—just in case."

"Us?" Maddie asked. "You mean you're not alone?"

Halt smiled at her. "Your father's here too," he said. Maddie whirled around to peer into the shadows of the stables, and he explained further. "Not *here* literally. He's in the village, posing as a Teutlandic knight. We got here a couple of days before you two arrived. I've been coming into the castle every day with my begging bowl to keep an eye on things."

"I saw you a few days ago. I thought there was something familiar about you," Maddie said. "But I wasn't expecting you to be here so I didn't recognize you."

"So how do you plan—" Will began, but Halt held up a hand to silence him. He had heard a noise from the upper floor of the stables. And now they saw a light moving at the top of the stairs that led down to the ground floor.

"It's the stablemaster," Halt whispered. "He must have heard something." He looked around quickly. The stall nearest the door was unoccupied. He gestured to it. "Hide in there while I take care of him."

21

Will and Maddie concealed themselves in the darkness of the empty stall while Halt moved farther into the stable, staying close to the line of stalls that were adjacent to the stairs. As he did, he could see the light growing stronger as the stablemaster made his way downstairs, grumbling and complaining to himself. The lantern swung in his hand, casting weird, moving shadows through the interior of the stable.

When Halt reached the last stall, opposite Bumper and Tug, he crouched beside the door, making a hand signal to the two horses. Seeing it, they began to nicker and whinny nervously, moving about in the cramped space of their stall, kicking against the timber door.

The stablemaster, hearing them, decided that it had been they who had disturbed his sleep. He snarled at them. "What's up with you two? Shut up, for pity's sake!"

He had obviously only just woken. Barefoot and wearing a long linen nightshirt, he crossed to their stall, holding his lantern high to light the interior, checking to see that there was nothing that had disturbed them. Maybe a cat or a dog had crept into the stables, and spooked the two small, shaggy horses. As he peered into their stall, he turned his back to Halt, who rose and approached behind him.

At the very last moment, the stablemaster sensed there was someone close to him and began to turn. But he was too late. An iron-hard arm clamped around his throat from behind. The stablemaster gave a short, startled gasp but it was cut off as the arm tightened, choking him.

He struggled wildly for a minute or so, but Halt's grip was relentless, tightening further and further, cutting off the air to the man's lungs. His struggles gradually became weaker and his movements more desperate. Then he sank down, limp and unconscious. Halt lowered him to the stable floor and straightened up, calling softly to his friends.

"All right, he won't cause any more trouble. Come and give me a hand tying him up."

Maddie and Will emerged from the shadows. Will quickly tied a stable cloth around the man's mouth to gag him, while Maddie studied the recumbent stablemaster where he lay on the straw-covered dirt floor of the stables.

"I didn't like the way he spoke to my horse," she said. There was a note of satisfaction in her voice.

"I'm sure he'll be more polite next time," Halt replied. Outside the stables they heard the gatehouse bell toll twice. "I want to get moving at six," Halt told them. "Maybe we'd better get some rest while we can."

"You do have a plan to get us out of here, haven't you?" Will asked. "I mean, you're not just making it all up as you go along, are you?"

"I'll explain in the morning," Halt said. "I've done enough talking for one night. And rescuing people like you is exhausting.

I need my sleep." He reached down and grabbed the stablemaster's collar. "Now give me a hand dragging this sleeping beauty into the stall."

Will reached down and took a hold of the man's nightshirt at the shoulders and together they heaved the limp figure into the empty stall, leaning him against the wooden wall.

Will regarded him critically. "He'll be cold when he wakes up."

"You're breaking my heart," Halt replied. But he relented and took a saddle blanket down from a peg at the back of the stall, draping it over the unconscious man.

Will sniffed. "Pongs a bit," he commented.

Halt looked at him, slightly exasperated. "Him or the blanket?" he queried.

Will grinned. "Both, probably."

They closed the door on the sleeping stablemaster and returned to the stall opposite. Halt settled down, pulling his cloak around him.

"You can take the first watch," he told Will, then looked at Maddie. "You take over at four bells and wake us at six."

And before they could argue, he closed his eyes and began breathing deeply. Will and Maddie exchanged a look. Will shrugged. After years of working with Halt, he was used to the older Ranger's gruff ways.

"I'll take the first watch," he echoed. "You wake us at six."

Maddie woke Will and Halt when she heard the gatehouse bell toll six times. Halt rummaged in his backpack and handed round a canteen of water and some strips of dried beef. They ate and drank morosely. The food would stem their hunger pangs, but it wasn't the most appetizing breakfast.

"You wouldn't have a flask of hot coffee instead, would you?" Will asked as he took a pull at the canteen.

"And some crispy hot bacon?" Maddie added.

Halt snorted derisively. "If I did, what makes you think I wouldn't keep it for myself?"

He rose and crossed to the stall where the stablemaster lay bound and gagged. He checked the man's restraints, making sure they were still tight, and that the gag wasn't impeding his breathing. The man's eyes glared at him above the gag and Halt shrugged.

"Some people don't know how to be grateful," he mused.

The stablemaster made an angry gurgling sound through the gag. Halt ignored him and returned to the stall where the others were waiting. He saw they had strung their bows and donned their saxes in their scabbards. Their quivers were clipped to their belts. The empty weapons case was discarded on the stall floor.

"He'll be fine," he said. "We might need to move him later so he's not in any danger."

"From what?" Maddie asked.

"The fire," Halt answered.

Will raised his eyebrows. "What fire might that be?"

"The one I'm going to light as a diversion, so you two can make it out through the gatehouse." He pointed to the two horses, who were waiting patiently. "I suggest you saddle up Bumper and Tug and get ready."

As they fetched their saddles and bridles from the pegs where they were hanging, Halt began winding the bark and burlap around his bow, disguising it once more. As he did, he elaborated on the escape plan.

"I'll pile up some damp straw near the doors and set fire to it. It should produce a lot of smoke and that will panic the horses in the stalls. Once there's a good deal of smoke, I'll let them out of their stalls and open the stable doors. They'll stampede out into the courtyard and, hopefully, head across the front of the keep, past the gatehouse."

"What if they don't?" Maddie asked.

Halt glanced at her. "They will, because you two will be riding at the back of the herd, driving them forward. Stay low in the saddle and you won't be noticed—at least, not in time for the guards to do anything to stop you. As you reach the gatehouse, swerve to your left and ride on through. With any luck, you'll take the guards by surprise. They won't see you until the last moment in all the confusion. Some of them may even leave their post to try to stop the horses. Just barge through any that are still in the gatehouse and ride on across the drawbridge and the causeway. There'll be nobody mounted and ready to pursue you so you should be able to get clean away. Horace will be waiting for you at the beginning of the village and he'll guide you from there."

"And what will you be doing?" Will asked.

Halt shrugged. "I'll wait for a little while, then follow you."

Will frowned thoughtfully as he considered the plan. "It all sounds a bit simple," he commented.

"Simple is good," Halt replied. "Clever is complicated, and complicated plans have an awkward tendency to go wrong."

Will opened his mouth to reply, then closed it again. Halt was right, he realized. A simple plan was often the best. If they could keep the horses bunched up and running, they would distract everyone's attention while Maddie and he made for the gate.

"You're right," he said, tossing Tug's saddle blanket across his back and then placing the saddle in position after it.

"I usually am," Halt replied, with maddening confidence. Then he made his way down toward the doors and began to heap together a pile of old, damp straw close by them. "Just be ready to go when I tell you," he called back softly.

Will glanced at Maddie, who had saddled Bumper while he was talking to Halt. She was stroking her horse's soft muzzle and all too obviously not grinning at the conversation she had just overheard.

"I've known him twenty years or more," Will said. "You can't win with him."

She nodded. "So I've noticed."

From the doorway, they heard the scraping sound of Halt's saxe on his flint. Bright sparks flew in the predawn darkness as he set a small pile of kindling alight, then placed it into the straw.

"Mount up," Halt called softly as the pile began to smolder. Already, some of the more restless horses in the stalls were beginning to whinny nervously as they smelled the acrid smoke.

Opening the door to their stall, Will led the way out, signing for Tug to follow. Maddie waited until the way was clear, then brought Bumper out as well. They swung up into the saddles. The noise from the other horses was increasing now as the smoke became thicker and they became increasingly disturbed. Will slung his bow over his shoulder and turned to Maddie.

"Stay low," he said. "And stay close."

22

THE SMOKE WAS GROWING THICKER AND THICKER AND Halt ran down the line of the stalls, unlatching the doors and letting the panicky occupants out into the open space at the center of the stables. The horses were whinnying and neighing loudly now as their anxiety increased. Instinctively, they knew the smell of smoke meant danger. They bunched up at the closed double doors, seeking a way out of the smoky interior—shoving and bumping one another, even occasionally snapping their big square teeth at any other horse that got in the way.

Even Tug and Bumper stirred uncertainly at the acrid smell of smoke. But their riders calmed them and kept the fidgeting and stamping to a minimum.

When he was satisfied that there was a dense cloud of smoke ready to escape, Halt unlatched the big double doors and threw them open, running to one side to avoid the stampeding horses as they charged out, skidding and slipping on the cobblestones of the courtyard.

"Fire!" he yelled at the top of his voice. "Fire in the stables!"

As he had foreseen, the leading horses went straight ahead

in their eagerness to escape the smoke, clattering into the clear space between the gatehouse and the entrance to the keep. Just to make sure, Will and Maddie brought up the rear, crouching low in their saddles and using their bows on the rumps of the horses near them, driving them forward. They, in turn, kept up the pressure on the leading horses, making sure they didn't deviate to left or right.

Startled cries rang out in the courtyard. There were only a few people out and about at this early hour, but they added to the noise and the confusion. The dense, choking cloud of smoke poured out of the stable after the stampeding horses.

Three of the gate guards ran into the courtyard, in an attempt to stop the charging herd. But they had no chance. One, the sergeant in command of the guard detail, ran in front of the panicked horses, waving his arms and shouting. But the lead horse, a black battlehorse, ran straight into him, buffeting him with its shoulder and knocking him to the ground. Frantic to evade the thundering hooves behind the battlehorse, the guard came to his hands and knees, scrabbling desperately at the cobblestones as he clawed his way to safety by the base of the wall. Seeing his fate, his two companions stopped, eyeing the galloping horses warily, not sure what to do.

Inside the gatehouse, the bell began to clang rapidly, sounding the alarm. People began to emerge from the keep and the four corner towers, most of them woken from sleep and only half dressed. Initially, they ran out into the courtyard to see what was happening. Then, as the stampeding horses lunged toward them, they reversed direction quickly, scrambling back to safety just in time. Other voices began to take up Halt's warning cry.

"Fire! Fire in the stables!"

Panic, confusion and uncertainty reigned. In those first moments, nobody had a clear idea of what action they should take. The guards on the battlements, safely above the plunging, rearing horses, looked down at the milling scene below them, not sure what they should do, waiting for someone in authority to issue orders.

In all this turmoil, Will and Maddie drew level with the main gate. They swerved to their left, staying low over their horses' necks, and galloped for the opening.

Tug's and Bumper's hooves clattered on the stones, echoing inside the confines of the gatehouse as they plunged down the short tunnel that led to freedom. The remaining guards, short-handed now that three of their number had run inside to try to stop the running horses, drew back to let them pass. One, more resolute than the others, realized that these two horses were carrying riders and stepped forward to try to stop them, holding his halberd up across his body to form a barrier.

It was a brave attempt, but a foolhardy one. Tug set his shoulder and thudded into the man, knocking the halberd from his grasp and sending him crashing against the stone wall of the gatehouse tunnel. Fortunately for the guard, he was wearing chain mail and a helmet, as his head slammed into the stonework. His eyes glazed and he slid down the wall, semiconscious.

The two horses plunged out into the morning sunlight, scattering the few early risers among the day visitors, who leaped to either side of the causeway to avoid the flashing, clattering hooves and hard-muscled bodies. Baskets of vegetables and joints of meat, intended for the chateau's kitchens, were scattered in the dust as the two horses plunged past, heading for the road to the village.

"They're getting away!" one guard yelled, regaining his feet and running to the outer gate to peer after the two riders.

"Who are getting away?" another queried, and the first guard stopped uncertainly.

"I don't know," he admitted. Then he gestured vaguely after the two rapidly disappearing horses and riders. "Them. Whoever they are."

Their sergeant, having picked himself up from where he had fallen, limped into the gatehouse, bruised and half dazed. Still, he was an old campaigner and he knew it was up to him to restore some form of order and discipline in the morning's chaos. He gestured to the heavy portcullis—a heavy iron grille that could be used to close off the entryway when the drawbridge was lowered.

"Let that down," he ordered. "Then go and try to stop those horses." He made his way into the guardroom set inside the gatehouse tower to rouse any members of the guard detail who might still be inside.

The guards moved to comply with his orders. They had just taken hold of the heavy wheel that raised and lowered the portcullis when a shambling figure in a green cloak hurried into the gatehouse.

"Just a minute!" he yelled fearfully. "Let me out of here!"

The guards paused, recognizing him. It didn't occur to either of them to question his unexpected presence. They assumed, in the confusion of the moment, that he had entered with the first of the early risers.

"Tomkin, are you all right?" one of them asked, releasing the windlass handle that raised and lowered the portcullis.

"All right? No, I'm not all right!" Tomkin—or rather Halt—replied in a rising falsetto of panic. "Those cursed horses nearly killed me! One trod on my foot as it went past! Now let me out of here!"

They waved him through, then resumed lowering the heavy gate as he hobbled quickly across the bridge and onto the causeway. As the panic began to subside, they grinned at each other, watching the indignant figure growing smaller in the distance.

"That put the wind up him, well and truly," said one.

Unfortunately for him, the sergeant chose that moment to reappear. "I'll put the wind up you, my lad, if you don't get that grille down in a hurry. And don't let anyone else through it!"

Inside the castle, order was gradually being restored. A fire-fighting party, armed with buckets of water and wet sacks, had made their way through the choking smoke cloud into the stables. There, they found that the fire was only a small matter. It was confined to a pile of damp, smoldering straw just inside the doors. They quickly extinguished it with half a dozen buckets of water.

The corporal in charge scratched his head. The smoldering straw had been piled up adjacent to the doors. Why would anyone in his right mind leave a pile of damp straw there? he wondered. One of his men, who had gone into the stable to look for any further danger, called to him, his voice urgent.

"Corporal! Better come and see this!"

"This" was the bound and muffled figure of the stablemaster, trussed up securely in an otherwise empty stall and wearing only his nightshirt. They hauled him to his feet and cut him loose. He spluttered and spat out a mouthful of old straw as they undid his gag.

"Who did this?" the corporal asked.

The stablemaster glared angrily. "It was that cursed beggar Tomkin!" he replied. "Don't let him get away!"

The corporal turned to one of his men. "Run to the gate-house and tell them to detain that old beggar!" he ordered.

The soldier nodded and ran off, his equipment and mail shirt jingling. He reached the gatehouse, a little out of breath, and passed on the corporal's message. The sergeant in command of the gatehouse guards turned an angry glare on two of his men.

"You let that old beggar go, didn't you?" he accused them.

The two men shuffled their feet awkwardly, not meeting his angry glare. "We didn't know, Sergeant—" one of them began.

The other joined in. "We had no orders to stop him," he offered.

The sergeant shook his head angrily. "You had no orders to let him go, either," he told them.

The first man spread his hands in a repentant gesture. "He was scared, Sergeant," he explained. "He'd nearly been trampled by those horses—"

The sergeant cut him off. "He was the one who set them loose!" he shouted, and the two guards cringed away from him. "And no wonder he was scared! He was behind the whole thing and he didn't want to get caught!"

"Was he with the other two?" the second guard asked, and instantly regretted the question as the sergeant swung on him, his eyes boring into him.

"Other two? What other two?" he demanded.

The guard refused to meet his gaze. "There were two riders with the stampeding horses. They swung through here and headed for the village," he said.

The sergeant's face reddened with anger, then began to turn pale again as he realized that someone would pay for this. Two mysterious riders had escaped from the castle. And he was the one in charge of security at the gate.

"Tell me about them," he said ominously.

23

IT TOOK SEVERAL HOURS FOR THE CASTLE HIERARCHY TO piece together the events of the morning, and to recognize the connection between the stable fire and the escape of the two prisoners from the northwest tower.

This was in large part due to the actions of two sergeants in the garrison. The commander of the gate guard decided to say nothing about the two unknown riders who had galloped out of the castle and headed across the causeway toward the village. This turned out to be an unfortunate choice on his part, but at the time, it seemed the wisest course.

The second sergeant in question was Ramon, the commander of the detail guarding Will and Maddie. As was his custom, he arrived at the tower room to check on the prisoners, and the guards in the corridor outside their room, shortly after half past seven o'clock.

He unlocked the heavy door and stepped inside. A jolt of panic struck him as he saw that the room was empty and the window was hanging open. One of the beds had been pulled against the wall beside the window.

With a glance at the sentries outside, to make sure they

couldn't see into the room, he closed the door behind him and moved to check the washroom and privy, finding nobody there. His pulse raced and he stood for several seconds, considering his next move. The open window seemed the only clue to the prisoners' disappearance and he crossed to it, leaning out and looking to either side, then up and down.

There was no clue as to where they had gone. The plasterwork that had been carried out left no handholds or footholds within reach of the window, yet somehow they must have gone out this way and climbed down. He noticed a gouge in the wooden frame of the window where Halt's arrow had struck it. The arrow itself was no longer there. Before leaving the night before, Will had dislodged it, broken it into half a dozen pieces and dropped it down the privy.

Ramon had no way of knowing whether the hole in the wood had been there before or if it was new. In any case, he couldn't see how it might have any connection to the missing prisoners. His breath came faster and he was close to panic. He was responsible for the two prisoners and he knew that Lassigny's vengeance would be vicious. A flogging would be the best he could hope for. But he'd seen Lassigny in a rage before and he knew it was possible that the Baron may sentence him to hang. His throat constricted at the thought, as if he could already feel the noose tightening around it. He paused for a few moments, thinking furiously. Then he came to a decision. He moved to the door, speaking in a loud voice back into the room as he opened it and stepped outside.

"The Baron wants to see you again. Be ready as soon as you've eaten."

He shut the door quickly, before the guards noticed there

was no reply. Then, turning to the three men waiting outside the door, he told them:

"You're not needed anymore. Take the day off."

The men murmured in pleasure at the news. They gathered their belongings and trooped down the stairs. Ramon listened to their boots clattering on the stone steps until the sound faded away. He took several deep breaths to steady his racing nerves, then, moving more deliberately than they had, he went down the stairs as well.

His own quarters were on the third floor of the tower, in a room he shared with two other sergeants. Neither of them was present when he entered. He took a knapsack from a peg beside his bed and hastily crammed some spare clothes and a few personal belongings into it. He took off the emblazoned surcoat that marked him as a member of the castle garrison and hung it on a peg on the wall. Then he donned an unmarked jerkin and swung a brown cloak around his shoulders, pulling the cowl up. Finally, he buckled on his sword in its scabbard—he was already wearing his heavy dagger—looked around the room, then opened the door and left.

He walked across the courtyard to the gatehouse, trying to appear casual and doing his best not to appear to be hurrying.

The portcullis had been raised; the guards had reopened it as there seemed to be no point in keeping it closed any longer. The gate sergeant was in his office beside the guardroom, having decided his best course would be to stay out of sight for as long as possible. One of the guards recognized Ramon and greeted him.

"Not on duty today?" he asked.

Ramon forced a grin. "I've got a free day," he said. "I'm heading for the tavern."

The guard shook his head ruefully. "Lucky you."

Ramon nodded and walked out across the drawbridge and onto the causeway. His back cringed and his muscles tensed as he waited for a shout from behind, ordering him back. He passed the halfway mark on the bridge and decided if such a call came, he would take to his heels and run.

But there was no shout from the gatehouse and he made his way off the bridge and onto the causeway. Increasing his pace, he headed for the village and the road away from Falaise. He was an experienced soldier and he'd have no trouble getting a position at another castle, in another barony. He might not be given the seniority he had here, nor would he be paid as well. But on the plus side, he would no longer have to endure Lassigny's sarcasm and cruelty to those who displeased him.

And Ramon knew that the man who had let the Araluens escape would displease Lassigny intensely.

Half an hour later, the two kitchen hands who brought Will and Maddie's breakfast found the corridor outside the prisoners' room empty and the door securely locked. There was no point knocking, as they knew the prisoners wouldn't be able to let them in. Shrugging and grumbling to themselves, they took the meal back to the kitchen.

When the cook saw them returning, he asked what had happened and they told him. Frowning, the cook took off his apron and tall hat and mounted the stairs, looking for Lassigny's seneschal. He found him in the Baron's office, going over the month's accounts with Lassigny.

"Your pardon, my lord," he said, after knocking and entering. "I need to speak to the seneschal." He was an excellent cook and he had no fear that the Baron might be annoyed by his interrupting them. He knew his ability in the kitchen would shield him from the outbursts of unreasoning rage for which Lassigny was well known. The Baron, eyes down on a row of figures, waved disinterestedly for him to proceed.

"I need to know, Sir Gaston, if the orders for the prisoners have been changed?"

Lassigny's eyes snapped up at the question. Lassigny had assumed the cook wanted to query some point about catering or kitchen supplies. Now his interest was galvanized.

"The prisoners?" he demanded. "What about them?"

The cook shrugged. "When my kitchen hands took them breakfast, the guards were gone and the door locked. Are we not feeding them anymore? If so, I need to know. I can't be wasting time—"

He was shoved aside by Lassigny as the Baron sprang from behind his desk and darted for the door, the seneschal following a few steps behind him. The two men pounded down the stairs and out into the courtyard, turning right to head for the northwest tower.

As the cook had reported, they found the guards gone and the room locked. Gaston had a key to the door and they opened it and stepped inside. It took mere seconds to ascertain that the prisoners had gone. Lassigny spat out a curse.

"Find Ramon," he ordered the seneschal, who hurried away. Lassigny raced back down the stairs and strode quickly to the gatehouse to confront the guards there. They stiffened to attention as he stormed into the short tunnel between the courtyard and the drawbridge.

"Where is your sergeant?" he demanded.

The guards exchanged nervous looks before one of them gestured to the office. "He's—"

The fuming Baron didn't allow him to finish. "Get him! Now!" he ordered, and the man, stumbling in his haste, half ran to the office door to summon his commander.

The sergeant stood before Lassigny, not meeting his eyes. The Baron was obviously furious and that was always dangerous for his underlings. Nervously, he stammered out an account of the fire in the stables and the subsequent stampede of the horses there, stressing that the fire was a minor blaze only and had been quickly extinguished.

"That's all?" Lassigny demanded. "You saw nothing of the two prisoners who escaped?"

"No, my lord," the sergeant lied. But one of his men contradicted him, hoping to be helpful.

"Two riders went out through the gate, Sergeant, remember? They were at the rear of the horses when they galloped past."

If looks could have killed, the sergeant's gaze would have withered the guard where he stood. Instead, Lassigny turned an ominously calm glare on the sergeant, who now broke out in a flood of nervous perspiration.

"Two riders went out through the gate?" he repeated. "What did they look like?"

"I . . . um, I nev . . . I never saw them, my lord," the sergeant managed to stammer.

Sir Gaston chose that moment to arrive, slightly out of breath after searching the sergeants' quarters in the northwest tower, then the garrison barracks in the keep.

"No sign of Ramon anywhere, my lord," he reported.

Lassigny turned on him, his fury boiling up once more.

"What do you mean no sign? He must be somewhere! Find him! Search the entire castle! Now!" he shouted.

Sir Gaston stood his ground. It would take hours to search the entire castle for one missing man and the Baron knew it. Again, the would-be helpful guard spoke nervously.

"Um . . . Sergeant Ramon left the castle half an hour ago, my lord," he quavered.

It was the last straw for Lassigny. He realized that Ramon had fled because he had allowed the prisoners to escape. He glared at Sir Gaston, his mouth working as he held back an enraged retort. He wanted to strike out at someone but he knew the seneschal was too valuable to him.

"Send men after them," he said. "There's only one road out of here and they'll be on it. Find them and bring them back."

"At once, my lord." Gaston turned to go, but the Baron held up a hand to stop him. Someone still had to be punished for this series of blunders. He pointed an accusing finger at the sergeant.

"Have him flogged," he said. Then, as the sergeant cringed away from him, he decided that wasn't enough. He swept the pointing finger around the small group of guards cowering before him. "Them too," he demanded. "All of them! And find those two cursed Rangers!"

24

Some hours before their escape was discovered, while the chateau's staff were busy rounding up the panicked horses, Will and Maddie cantered easily across the causeway, heading for the road into the village of Falaise. It was Maddie's inclination to go faster, but Will held their pace back to a smooth lope.

"If we gallop at full speed, we'll be noticed. People will either remember us or try to stop us," he told her. "Better to take it easy and avoid arousing suspicion."

So they maintained their easy pace through the traffic that was heading for the castle. As they came closer to the outskirts of the village, they saw a tall figure astride a battlehorse waiting by the side of the road. Maddie's heart leaped in her chest as she recognized her father, in spite of the red surcoat bearing a black bear on the left breast.

"Goot mornink," he said as they drew rein beside him. "It iss goot to zee you."

Maddie frowned at him as he grinned. "That is the worst Teutlandic accent I have ever heard," she said.

His grin widened. "I t'ought it vas priddy goot," he replied.

Then, in a normal voice, he said, "This isn't a good place to sit around talking. Follow me."

He set his heels to his horse and cantered into the village, staying to the right of the high street. The two Rangers followed him, riding in single file so as not to impede traffic coming in the opposite direction.

After they had gone fifty meters, he swung off the high street into a side lane on their right. They followed him down the narrow thoroughfare, lined either side by low, single-story houses constructed in wattle and daub and roofed with thatch. There was barely enough room for two horses to pass side by side. Thirty meters down this narrow path, they came to a cross street, somewhat wider and running parallel to the high street. Horace turned left here and they followed him. Glancing farther down the lane as they turned, Maddie could see there was one more cross street running parallel to the one they were now in. After that, the village tailed off into fields planted with crops, and open pasture where cattle and horses grazed.

They continued for several hundred meters along the cross road, then Horace turned left into another narrow lane and they followed him. He drew rein outside a small house, similar to the others around it, and dismounted. He dragged the side gate open, allowing them to enter the yard behind the house.

There was a small, open-sided stable and a washroom and privy in the yard. As Maddie dismounted, she hurled herself at Horace, embracing him fiercely.

"Oh, Dad! It's so good to see you!" she cried. He hugged her back, a huge lump in his throat preventing him from speaking for several seconds. Will stood by, watching them and grinning.

Finally, Horace managed to speak. His voice came out as a

croak. "I've been so worried about you," he said, disengaging from the hug and looking fondly down at her. "I thought I'd die myself when I watched you fight that knight."

She made a dismissive gesture. "Him? He was no trouble at all."

He shook his head in disbelief. "A fully armed and armored knight, with a four-meter lance? No trouble at all? Of course not."

"Well," she said, "maybe he was a little bit of trouble. But I knew Bumper would look after me."

While they had been greeting each other, Will had unsaddled Bumper and Tug and led them to the stable. Abelard, who was already ensconced there, whinnied a greeting and they responded. He moved aside to allow them access to the feed bin, which was half full of hay. They munched hungrily. Will patted Bumper's rump as he began eating and smiled at his best friend and his apprentice.

"I suppose he did," he agreed. "He is the brains in your partnership, after all."

He moved forward and clasped hands with Horace, then pulled the taller man into a tight bear hug.

"Truth be told," he said, "you were worried about what Cassandra would do to you if Maddie were injured. I know I was."

Horace nodded ruefully. "I could see a lifetime of misery stretching before me. The words *this is all your fault* echoed in my brain." He gestured toward the back door leading into the house. "Come on in. We've got coffee here and I'll wager you're ready for a cup."

"Am I?" Will said. "We've had nothing but water for the past few days. You get that organized while I unsaddle your horse."

Horace dropped his arm around Maddie's shoulders and led

her into the house, while Will began unsaddling his battle-horse. Stamper looked a little bewildered at the sudden crowd of small, shaggy Ranger horses that now shared his stable. But he accepted the new arrivals without any rancor. He was used to working with Ranger horses and held them in a certain respect.

Inside the house, Horace had stoked the fire into flames and filled the blackened coffeepot with water from the large jug he had filled earlier that morning at the village pump. He hung the pot from a hinged iron arm and swung it in so that it was over the fire.

Maddie took a seat by the table and looked around the small, low-roofed room. There were two narrow beds along the wall, two armchairs by the fire and the table and chairs where she was sitting. Apart from that, there was no furniture. But the open fire kept the space warm and comfortable, and two large windows along the alley-side wall let in plenty of light. The windows were unglazed but they could be closed by hinged shutters.

The water boiled and Horace had just measured a generous amount of coffee into the pot when Will entered. The aroma of brewing coffee filled the little one-room house and he sniffed it appreciatively.

"Oh, that's good!" he said. He glanced at the narrow shelf over the fireplace that served as a larder. "I trust you have honey?"

Horace grinned. "Of course," he said. He checked the coffee-pot, swinging the hinged arm out from the fire, and stirred it gently. Then he placed it on the table and fetched two mugs. He set them down beside the pot.

"Help yourselves," he said. "We only have two mugs, so I'll

wait." He placed the jar of honey and an iron spoon on the table, knowing this would be Will's next request, and watched as the two Rangers sweetened their coffee, then drank eagerly.

"Now what on earth was behind that duel with Lassigny's henchman?" he asked. He and Halt had known that the duel had been organized, of course, but they had no idea why.

Will shrugged. "We think Lord Anthony was right when he said Lassigny might have designs upon Araluen. He was very eager to know about the Ranger Corps and Araluen's defenses, and we thought the duel might be a way of showing him that an attack wasn't in his best interests."

"Particularly," Maddie chipped in, "if one of his knights was defeated by a mere girl."

Horace turned a critical eye on Will. "You didn't think it would do the job if you were the one to fight him?"

Will glanced sidelong at Maddie. "She got in first," he said. Horace snorted, and Will continued. "You know how stubborn the women in your family can be when they set their minds to something."

Horace had to nod agreement at that. Maddie was her mother's daughter in so many ways, he reflected. "So, what do we do now?" he asked.

"I say we leave the Gallicans to stew in their own juice and get the blazes out of here. Let's get back to Araluen."

"I couldn't agree more," Horace said. "We'll get going tomorrow."

Maddie said nothing for a few moments. She looked thoughtfully at the table.

"Maybe we should wait a few days," she said finally.

Both men looked at her in utter disbelief.

"Wait a few days?" Horace exclaimed. "What are you talking about?"

She pursed her lips and shrugged. "They'll be expecting us to make a run for it, surely," she said. "Lassigny will have men out on all the roads looking for us. I thought if we stayed out of sight for a few days, we could let the hue and cry die down."

Horace nodded slowly, seeing the sense of her suggestion. "It might be a good idea at that," he said.

But Will was watching Maddie shrewdly. He sensed she had something else on her mind, something she wasn't saying. But he knew her well enough to realize that it would be useless pushing her to reveal what it might be. As he had told Horace, the women in his family were renowned for their stubbornness.

There was silence in the room for a minute or so. Then they heard the sound of running feet in the lane outside. A shadow passed across one of the windows, then the door latch rattled and the door flew open.

Halt dashed inside and slammed the door behind him. He took the heavy locking beam from where it leaned against the wall beside the door and dropped it into place, securing the door against any attempt to enter.

Before any of the startled group could speak, he jerked his thumb in the direction of the high street.

"Lassigny's finally got his men organized," he told them. "They're searching the village. We've got maybe ten minutes before they get here."

25

Everyone began to speak at once, but Horace raised a hand for silence.

"There's no cause for alarm," he said. "Halt says we've got ten minutes. That's plenty of time to get ready." He began to redon the red surcoat he had been wearing, then he buckled his sword belt around it. He still wore his mail shirt and the coif was gathered about his shoulders. "Let's see how the Baron's men cope with an angry Teutlandic knight when they disturb him," he said.

The others fell silent, waiting to follow his lead. He pointed to the rear door of the house, which led to the small stable yard.

"You lot wait out there," he said.

Maddie frowned at him. "There's no place for three of us to hide out there," she pointed out. "And there are four horses out there as well. Even if we could hide, they'll raise suspicions if they're seen."

Horace shook his head. "They're not going to be seen," he assured her. "And the searchers are not going to see you. They're not getting any farther than that front door. Now go."

He made a brushing gesture with his hand. Halt nodded and took Maddie's arm, leading her toward the rear door. She went reluctantly at first. Then she saw that Will was following and decided that perhaps her father was in charge of this situation. She stopped resisting and allowed herself to be led out into the stable yard behind the house. Will was the last to go and he closed the door behind him.

Horace took a deep breath. He slid the sword a few centimeters out of its scabbard, checking that it was free to move, then let it fall back into place. He stepped to the door and removed the locking bar, then laid his hand on the latch.

From the street outside, he could hear shouts and angry voices, and the sound of heavy fists thumping on doors. He pictured in his mind's eye how Lassigny's men would pound heavily on a door, then shove it violently inward when it was opened, pushing occupants aside and barging in to search for the missing prisoners. He smiled grimly. They'd have a surprise waiting for them when they banged on this door, he thought.

He heard the shouting and banging come closer, until the searchers were at the house across the alley. Angry, raised voices were audible as the householder objected and was shoved roughly aside. The houses were small and it took only a minute or so to ascertain that nobody was hidden in them. The door across the way banged open again, and heavy footsteps approached the door behind which Horace was waiting.

BANG! BANG! BANG! A mailed fist slammed on the warped timbers of the door, rattling it against the frame.

A rough voice shouted, "Open in the name of—"

Horace went into action. He slammed the door open in a violent movement and thrust himself out into the street, surprising the soldier who was demanding entry. The reaction was so quick and so violent that the soldier, one of a party of three, recoiled instinctively, then was shouldered out of the way by Horace's tall, well-muscled frame as he charged out of the house, his face a mask of fury.

"What is it?" he shouted angrily. "What do you want?"

His hand was on the sword hilt and he withdrew the blade several centimeters, ready to draw it and start laying about him. The searchers were encumbered by the fact that they were carrying spears. Their swords were in their scabbards and the angry knight bustled them, crowding them so they had no room to use the long weapons. They gave ground, moving farther out into the lane and he followed, still shouting.

"Who are you? How dare you disturb me! I'll have your ears for this!"

He made no attempt to employ the fake Teutlandic accent. This was a serious matter and he needed to put the soldiers off guard and on the defensive. A silly accent wouldn't help him do that. Instead, he ranted and shouted and threatened.

The three soldiers, seeing a furious knight in a foreign livery, quailed before him. It was one thing to threaten simple villagers, quite another to antagonize a big, armed warrior who was obviously already furious at being disturbed.

"Apologies," the first soldier said, touching his hand to his forehead in a salute. "We're searching for—"

He got no further. Horace thrust his face a few centimeters from the soldier's and roared at the top of his voice.

"I am Sir Wilhelm of Starkhaus!" he bellowed. "A knight of the Teutlandic court! How dare you address me like that? You will call me Sir Wilhelm, or sir. Or my lord!"

"Uh . . . ah . . . yes, my lord . . . ," the soldier stammered. He thought it best to use the most impressive of the titles suggested.

"Please forgive us, my lord . . . Sir Wilhelm . . . we have orders to—"

"Orders?" Horace interrupted. "Whose orders?"

"Baron Lassigny's orders, my lord," the soldier replied, continuing to back away a pace at a time.

"Never heard of him!" Horace replied haughtily. The soldier gestured uncertainly in the direction of the castle.

"He's the lord of the Chateau des Falaises, my lord," the soldier replied, stumbling slightly over the repetition of the word *lord*. "He's ordered us to search for two foreign spies—"

"Are you calling me a spy?" Horace demanded, his voice rising in pitch and volume. He drew his sword with a ringing shriek of metal on metal, bringing it up so that the tip was resting just below the soldier's nose. Hastily, the soldier gave more ground, his eyes fixated on the gleaming metal blade.

"No, my lord! Of course not! I—"

"I am here quite openly, wearing my surcoat and displaying my coat of arms! And now you accuse me of being a spy! Me, Sir Wilhelm of Starkhaus! One of the most prominent knights at the Teutlandic court! You say I'm a spy? I could kill you for this insult, and your Baron—whoever he is—would agree that I was within my rights!"

The soldier had an uneasy feeling that the big, angry Teutlander was right. Nobles and knights tended to stick together in matters like this—even if they were from different countries. And the furious knight was correct: He was not skulking and hiding his identity. He was openly displaying his coat of arms and proclaiming his position to the world.

"Please, my lord, forgive me!" he babbled desperately. "No

such insult was intended! The spies are Araluens. They escaped from the chateau early this morning. The Baron is furious. He had the gatehouse guards flogged and sent the rest of us to search for the escapees."

Horace lowered the sword, and the soldier, who had become cross-eyed staring at the razor-sharp tip, shook his head as the focus point for his staring eyes was removed. After a pause, Horace returned the sword to its scabbard, slamming it home. The soldier breathed a sigh of relief.

"Well, they're not here," Horace said, lowering the volume from a shout but still keeping it louder than normal conversation level.

The soldier pointed nervously at the door behind him. "Perhaps if we could see—"

Horace went back up to a shout in a flash, as his hand went back to the hilt of his sword. "You doubt my word?" he roared. "You, a minion, a mere lackey of this Lassernay person?"

"Lassigny, my lord," the soldier corrected him.

"I don't give a fiddler's curse what his name is! You have insulted my honor! You have called me a liar! And you will pay for this grave insult! I am a senior knight of the Teutlandic court and you have insulted me!"

For a moment, Horace wondered if he might be overdoing the "senior knight of the Teutlandic court" but it still seemed to be impressing the soldier before him.

"Not at all, sir . . . my lord! Please, no insult was intended. Of course there's no need for us to see inside the house! Your word as a senior knight of the"—he hesitated, then regained the full title—"Teutlandic court . . . is more than sufficient proof for me! And for the Baron!"

Horace folded his arms over his chest, allowing his anger to appear mollified.

"What is your name?" he demanded arrogantly.

The soldier hesitated. The last thing he wanted was for this knight to deliver a complaint about him to the Baron. He decided to lie. His name was Gaspard Allende but he gave the name of one of his friends instead.

"I am called Hercule, my lord. Hercule Lombard. I am a corporal in the guard." He turned his shoulder to display the corporal's chevrons on his upper sleeve. Horace pretended to study them for a few seconds, as if committing the name to memory. Then he spoke again, resuming a more subdued voice, but lacing it with overtones of sarcasm.

"So tell me, *Corporal* Hercule Lombard, you say these Araluen spies escaped earlier this morning?"

"That's right, my lord. They started a fire in the—"

Irritably, Horace waved him to silence. "I don't care *how* they managed to escape," he said. "Although, if your performance is typical of the castle guard, I'm not surprised that they did."

Allende hung his head sheepishly. "No, my lord," he muttered.

Horace continued. "But if, as you say, they escaped this morning—several hours ago—why would they possibly stop here in the village?"

Allende opened his mouth to reply, realized that what the Teutlander said made sense, and shut it again. Eventually, he found his voice.

"Um . . . I suppose they wouldn't, my lord," he admitted.

Horace nodded several times. "Exactly. If they had escaped, they would undoubtedly have kept riding and headed for home—back to Araluen?"

"Indeed they would, my lord," Allende admitted.

"While you waste time here, annoying me?"

"Yes, sir," Allende replied miserably.

Horace leaned toward him, thrusting his face close to the other man's. "Then I suggest you tell this to your Baron"—he hesitated as if forgetting the name once more—"Lasserboo."

"It's Lassigny, sir," Allende corrected him.

Horace roared once more in fury. "Do I look as if I *care?*"

The corporal stepped back hurriedly once more and came to attention. "No, sir! My apologies, sir!"

Horace made an irritable gesture of dismissal with his right hand. "Then get out of my sight and leave me alone!" he ordered.

The corporal looked around, saw his two companions, who had shrunk back against the house opposite, trying not to attract the attention of the furious knight, and gestured for them to follow him.

"Yes, sir! At once, sir! Leaving now, sir!"

Horace watched them depart hurriedly up the alley, smiled to himself and opened the door to the small house, stooping to enter under the low lintel.

He stopped in the middle of the room and the rear door opened, admitting his three friends. They burst into spontaneous applause.

"Oh, well done, Sir Wilhelm," Halt said.

Horace came to attention, clicked his heels resoundingly and bowed stiffly from the waist. "You could hear that—from the stable yard?" he asked.

Maddie grinned. "I imagine they could hear that from the chateau."

26

Halt was in the small washroom at the rear of the house, vigorously applying a pair of shears to his mass of long white hair. He normally kept his hair and beard close cropped but had grown it longer for his role as Tomkin, the itinerant beggar. Now that Tomkin would no longer be needed, he took the first opportunity to cut his hair short again.

He heard the door to the house open and quickly hid the shears under a hand towel, drawing his saxe in the same movement. He grabbed a handful of hair and held it out from his head, sawed through it with the saxe and discarded it onto the flagstone floor.

It had long been rumored around Castle Redmont that Halt cut his hair and beard with his saxe. In truth, he had always used a pair of shears, but his tonsorial skills were sadly lacking and the result was always rough and uneven. For this reason he had fostered the myth that he used a saxe, allowing it to gain credence. Nobody would expect a tidy result if he did it that way, whereas if word got around that he used shears, people might make fun of his lack of skill.

"So it's true?" said Horace behind him, with a note of wonder.

Halt wheeled about to face his friend, the saxe in his right hand and a glare on his face.

"You *do* use a—" Horace gestured toward the gleaming saxe, then stopped as he noticed the angry expression on Halt's face. "I mean you . . . ah . . . never mind," he finished weakly. He changed the subject. "We thought we should discuss our next move."

Halt nodded. "Good idea. I'll be a few minutes." He raised the saxe again and seized another clump of hair, holding it taut for the gleaming blade. Horace nodded several times, then turned on his heel and went back into the house. Halt smiled grimly, retrieved the shears and went back to clipping his hair and beard.

He gave it a few more minutes, then studied the result. Satisfied that it was no better or worse than normal, he ran his fingers through his hair, shaking out the last few cut strands. Then he stowed the shears away and went into the house.

"I tell you it's true," Horace was saying as Halt entered. "He does use his sa—" He heard the door and stopped talking.

Will smiled. He had lived with Halt for five years during his apprenticeship and knew the secret of his old mentor's haircuts. But he had kept the facts a secret, as Halt had requested. Maddie, however, was studying the old Ranger's hair and beard with great interest.

She dragged her eyes away as Halt came farther into the room, looking curiously at Horace.

"Who uses what for what?" Halt asked.

Horace made a disclaiming gesture with both hands. "Nobody. It's nothing. Just idle gossip."

"Always a waste of time," Halt said. He noticed the coffeepot hanging on the arm over the coals, swung it out and lifted it to test its weight. Satisfied that it was half full, he poured himself a cup and sat at the table, spooning honey into the fragrant liquid.

"So, what's our next move?" he asked.

Will shifted to a more comfortable position in his armchair by the fire. "We thought we should wait here for a few days. Sending men to search the village was a knee-jerk reaction on Lassigny's part. Given time to think about it, he's certain to realize it made no sense and cast his net wider. He'll send men out along the roads to La Lumiere and the coast. They're the most likely routes we'd follow. We'll wait for them to come back, then we'll head out once it's safe."

"In the meantime," Horace added, "Will and Maddie should stay out of sight in the house here."

Halt nodded. "Sounds reasonable," he said. He looked around the room, studying his companions. "I take it we're all agreed?"

Will and Horace nodded emphatically.

Halt noticed that Maddie was hesitating. "Maddie?" He cued her for a response.

She waited a few more seconds before committing herself, then she said uncertainly, "I'm not so sure."

Will glanced at her curiously. Earlier, he had noticed that she had held back when their departure had been mooted. "You think we should go right away?"

She shook her head as she came to a decision. "I think we should finish what we set out to do," she said.

Halt nodded. He too had noticed her earlier hesitation and he had an idea as to what she might be thinking. He respected her skill as a tactician and her ability to sum up a situation and come up with a course of action. She might be young, he thought, but she had a good head on her shoulders. In addition, she was her mother's daughter. And Cassandra had always had a shrewd and agile mind.

"Go on," he prompted.

But before she could, Horace reacted in surprise. "You think we should make another attempt to rescue Prince Giles?" he said incredulously.

Maddie, committed now, set her jaw in a firm line. "Yes. I do."

Horace shook his head in disbelief. "We've just got you out of that castle. Now you want to go back in?"

"Yes, I do," she repeated.

Horace looked at Halt and Will, hoping for them to share his disbelief and disapproval. However, he was disappointed. Both men seemed to be considering Maddie's statement.

"Am I the only sane one here?" he demanded.

Will pursed his lips thoughtfully before answering. "I think she may have a point," he said.

Horace was speechless. Maddie glanced at Will and nodded her gratitude. He gestured for her to elaborate on her idea. She mustered her arguments for a few seconds, then spoke.

"We've agreed that Lassigny will assume we're long gone, heading back to La Lumiere or to Araluen . . ." She paused and they all nodded. "Then the very *last* thing he'd expect is that we'd go back into the chateau to fetch Giles out. In a way, it could be the safest place for us to be."

Will shook his head. "I don't think you could ever assume that the chateau would be a safe place for us," he said, and she held up a hand in agreement.

"Very well. That might be overstating the case. *Safe* is probably the wrong word to use. There are too many suspicious eyes in there. But it is a fact that he would hardly expect to see us back there. And if he's not looking out for us, then there might be an opportunity to rescue Giles and get him back to his father."

She paused and looked around at the three faces. She could see that nobody was actually disagreeing with her. Halt and Will were both nodding thoughtfully as they considered her words. Horace was less enthusiastic but at least he wasn't offering any argument against her line of thinking. She pushed her case a little harder, speaking directly to Will.

"After all, we did take on this mission. I'd like to see us complete it. And while Giles didn't strike me as the most impressive character in the world, I think he deserves better than to be left as a prisoner."

"That's true," Will said. "And I'd quite like to give Lassigny another smack in the eye."

"I have to admit that is an attractive idea," Maddie replied. "He was very patronizing and very arrogant and I'd enjoy taking him down a peg or two."

"And if Giles is returned to his father, that will make Philippe's position more secure. And that in turn will lessen any threat that Lassigny might pose to Araluen," Halt pointed out.

The three Rangers exchanged nods, then turned to face Horace, waiting for him to voice an opinion. The tall warrior sighed and nodded in turn, although reluctantly.

"Everything you say makes sense," he admitted. "But none of you is married to Cassandra. Where her daughter is concerned, good sense just melts away."

"The next question is, how do you plan to get back inside the chateau?" Halt said. "If Lassigny had the gate guards flogged, whoever's on duty now is going to be right on their toes. They may have become complacent about who goes in and out, but that won't be the case now."

"We'll have to find another way in," Maddie agreed.

There was a silence in the room for a few moments, then Will said, "The walls are too high and too exposed to climb over them. We'd be spotted for sure."

"And even if we made it in, we'd never get Giles out that way," Maddie added, remembering the terror on Giles's face when they had to force him out the window and haul him up one floor in the tower.

"There's sure to be another way in," Will said.

Halt looked sidelong at him. "That's a very confident statement about an impregnable castle," he said. "After all, nobody seems to have found an alternative way in for years. What if there isn't another way?"

Will took a sip of his coffee and met his old mentor's gaze.

"There'll be another way," he said. "We just have to find it."

27

THE FOUR FRIENDS STOOD TO ONE SIDE OF THE ROAD LEAD-
ing onto the causeway, studying the chateau and the rocky outcrop on which it was built. They were dressed in nondescript
farmworkers' clothes that Halt had picked up in the village
market—blue cotton smocks over coarse woolen trousers, with
wide-brimmed, floppy straw hats pulled low to hide their faces.

Far below them, the waves, whipped up by the brisk wind,
crashed against the rocks, surging into the narrow channel
between the mainland and the small rocky islet on which the
castle was built, then bursting into tall columns of spray as the
constricted water finally met up with the rocks at the base of
the causeway.

Below them, midway along the far side of the channel, gulls
wheeled in circles, screaming their annoyance at one another and
swooping down from time to time toward a discolored pile of
garbage that lay at the edge of the rock, gradually being washed
into the lake by the action of the waves.

As they watched, a new consignment surged out of a small
hole five meters up the rock face, rolling and slithering down to
add itself to the pile already there.

A few seconds later, a discharge of water followed, as the castle workers emptied a barrel into the garbage chute to flush away any residue that might have been caught up.

"There's your way in," Will said. "I noticed it when we first arrived."

Maddie wrinkled her nose, although the rubbish pile was too far away for her to be able to smell it.

"It's a rubbish chute," she said.

Will nodded. "It is. Fortunately, it's not a sewer outlet. That's farther along." And indeed, when she looked in the direction he indicated, Maddie could see another outlet among the rocks, stained and discolored with the residue of what had been dumped out of it and had failed to wash completely away.

"I see what you mean," she said.

Will pointed to the rubbish chute. "It must lead up into the cellars somewhere," he said. "Probably underneath the keep. That's where the kitchens are. Somebody could climb up there and bypass the castle's defenses."

"So why hasn't an invading force done that before?" Maddie asked.

Will shrugged. "It's an exposed spot. If you tried to get a large party of men up that way, or even a small one, they'd be seen and the garrison could simply wait and take them one by one as they emerged at the other end of the pipe." He paused. "But one person could probably manage it without being seen— particularly at night."

"And who might that one person be?" Maddie asked, her gaze traveling round the other three.

Halt made a negative gesture with his hands. "Not me. I'm too old to go slithering up garbage chutes," he said.

"And I'm too big," Horace added. "I'd probably get stuck halfway up and that would be no use at all."

Maddie's questioning gaze stopped at Will. "That leaves you and me," she said.

Will shrugged and smiled. "And what's the first rule between masters and apprentices?" he asked her.

She heaved a deep sigh. "If a job is dirty and unpleasant or uncomfortable, it's a job for the apprentice," she replied.

He nodded emphatically. "That's certainly the way I remember it," he said. "So all you need to do is swim across that inlet—it's no more than ten meters wide—climb the chute, find Giles and bring him out the same way."

"Down the rubbish chute?" she asked.

"Unless you can think of another way, yes."

"That'll be fun," she said, remembering how Giles had balked at the idea of being hauled up one floor of the tower on the end of a rope. "He's not the most adventurous type, after all."

Will considered the point for several seconds and realized she was right. "Maybe you can just get him to the top of the chute and give him a good shove," he suggested.

"That might do it," Maddie agreed doubtfully.

Will spread his hands in a helpless gesture. "I can't be expected to think of everything," he said. "I've come up with the master plan. It's up to you to look after the minor details."

Halt snorted derisively. "Some minor detail!" he said. "Just the small matter of how you get the prince out of the castle, which is the object of the whole exercise."

Maddie gnawed on her thumb, thinking the matter over for some time. "I guess I can manage it," she said at length. "Even if I have to bring him out at knifepoint."

Horace had been watching them throughout this discussion. Now he decided to join in. "What if you find that the rubbish chute doesn't lead to the basement?" he asked. "It might well open into the courtyard itself, in full view. Or it might be barred."

"In that case, Maddie turns around, comes back out and we go home. But at least we'll have tried to complete the mission," Will said. He paused, then added, "Do you have a better idea?"

Gloomily, Horace agreed that he did not. Will spread his hands out in a so-that's-it gesture. He looked at Halt. "How about you?"

The older Ranger shook his head. "No. It seems like the best way to me," he admitted.

"Just one thing," Horace remonstrated. "You seem to be quite prepared to put my daughter into more danger—sending her back into that chateau."

Will eyed him with a level gaze for a few seconds before answering. "She's a Ranger," he said simply.

Horace's eyes dropped from his as he emitted a deep sigh. "You're right," he said. "But I don't have to like it."

Maddie studied her father. She could understand his reluctance at seeing her going into harm's way, but it seemed to her that he was applying a double standard. After all, he'd been putting himself into dangerous situations all his life, and it didn't seem to occur to him that she or her mother might worry about him.

"I'll be fine, Dad," she told him, resting a hand on his forearm. "As Will says, I'm a Ranger and it's my job."

He shook himself and straightened up, dispelling the despondency that had come over him. "All right," he said in a brisker tone. "When do we do it?"

Will glanced up at the sun. It was early afternoon. "Tonight would be as good a time as any," he said. "Lassigny's search parties are still out on the road looking for us, so the garrison will be short-handed."

Maddie nodded. Now that a course of action had been agreed, she was keen to get on with it as soon as possible.

"Tonight it is then," she said.

Maddie and Will picked their way carefully through the tumble of rocks at the base of the causeway. Will wore his cloak, with the cowl pulled up to hide his face. Maddie wore a dark pullover jacket with a hood that served the same purpose.

Will's bow was slung over his shoulder and his quiver was clipped to his belt under the cloak. Maddie's saxe and throwing knife were on her belt. In addition, a pouch of rocks hung at her waist and her sling was coiled and secured around her left forearm.

Horace had wanted to accompany them but Halt and Will vetoed the idea.

"Will and Maddie are used to moving without being noticed," Halt told the tall knight. "You tend to crash around like a bear in a bad mood." He smiled. "No offense," he added.

Horace gave him a long, hard look. "I've noticed that when people say that, they tend to be very offensive," he said.

Halt shrugged.

Will tried to smooth matters over. "Regardless," he said, "the fewer people there are milling around the base of the cliff, the less chance there is that someone will spot us."

Horace grunted assent. He could see that Will was right. Truth be told, he knew that Halt was right too. Rangers were trained to move silently and unobtrusively. Knights weren't. He knew the older Ranger made sense, but he didn't have to like it. But then, he realized, Halt had never been known for his tact.

Originally, the rocky outcrop on which Chateau des Falaises was sited had been an island, separated from the mainland by a narrow channel. The channel had been filled in at the point where the causeway was built to provide access to the chateau's drawbridge and entry. The tide surged in and out of the narrow channel now, the water rising and falling as it did so. Will suspected that there was a culvert underneath the causeway, allowing some of the tidal surge to pass through and get away. That meant there could be strong currents beneath the surface.

They moved away from the causeway, to a point opposite the rubbish chute, where the channel narrowed, leaving a mere ten meters for Maddie to cross. It was a shorter distance, but they both knew that if there were an undertow, it would be stronger here where the channel narrowed.

"Remember the current," he said in a whisper. Will had already warned Maddie of this possibility when they were getting ready earlier in the day, but the last thing he wanted was for the girl to be swept into a tunnel under the cliffs. Maddie nodded.

"Here's a good spot," he said, and they stopped.

Maddie stripped off her outer garments until she wore only a light shift and a pair of cotton shorts. Will took her dark outer garments and wrapped them inside a waterproof oiled cloth, along with her boots, knife belt, shot pouch and a towel. He tied a light cord to the bundle.

"I'll toss it to you when you're across," he said.

Maddie nodded and stepped carefully down the unseen

rocks to the water's edge. She crouched down and lowered her-self into the water, gasping instinctively and then realizing that the water temperature was actually several degrees warmer than the air. She took two paces and the water rose to her chin, the current tugging at her and the surge of the water threatening to pull her off balance. She glanced up at Will, a dark shadow against the night sky. He raised his hand in a gesture that was half wave, half blessing.

She turned toward the chateau and pushed off with her feet, using the strength of her leg muscles to give her impetus, and swam smoothly toward the other side.

28

MADDIE SLITHERED OUT OF THE WATER ONTO THE ROCKS, shivering as the night air struck her wet body. Will had been right, she thought to herself. There was a strong current running below the surface and it had tried to drag her toward the causeway. But the crossing was short and she had fought against it, drifting only a few meters to her right.

"Rope's coming," Will called softly to her.

She heard the line slap against the rocks behind her and groped for it, pulling the watertight bundle across the narrow channel and hauling it up onto the rocks. Hastily, she undid the line securing it and opened the package. She took up the towel that was inside and quickly dried herself, then redonned her outer clothes over the wet shift and shorts that she wore. Once she was dressed, she belted on the double scabbard holding her saxe and her throwing knife, slung her shot pouch over her shoulder and wound the sling around her left wrist.

There was another item in the package—a metal mesh cage holding a length of candle inside it to use as a lantern. A flint, a small tinderbox and several spare candles were included. She put them in the side pocket of her pullover and clambered up the uneven slope to the mouth of the garbage chute, wincing as she stepped through the accumulated garbage on the rocks. The smell was strong as she disturbed the rotting waste and she slipped once or twice before she reached the dark hole in the rocks. She turned and looked back. On the far side, she could just make out Will's dark shape, crouched among the boulders. She waved once, then crawled up into the tunnel.

The fetid smell was even stronger once she was in the tunnel. She paused to tie her kerchief over her mouth and nose, and began breathing through her open mouth. She took out her flint and tinderbox once she was concealed from any eyes that might be watching from the castle walls. The flint would make a vivid flash that would be easily seen, even from a distance. She scraped it along the blade of her saxe and let the resulting shower of sparks fall into a small handful of tinder. The sparks caught and a small tongue of flame flickered up. She placed it against the candlewick, then closed the front window of the lantern.

The yellow light illuminated the interior of the tunnel for several meters. It was an irregular circle in shape; the rock sides showed the gouges of the picks and crowbars that had formed it, although any sharp edges had been worn away by decades of use and the constant flushing with water. The tunnel sloped up and to her right, heading in the general direction of the keep, she thought. That was as they had imagined it would be. It made sense for the garbage disposal chute to be near the kitchens, which were located in the basement of the keep. The tunnel was a tight fit, with only centimeters to spare around her shoulders. Holding the lantern before her, she began to crawl upward on her elbows and knees, the little yellow flame lighting up the interior of the tunnel for three or four meters in front of her before the darkness swallowed it. Her world was confined to a short tube of rough-hewn rock, littered here and there with old and rotting pieces of vegetables, meat bones and other items that she chose not to inspect too closely.

"Dad was right. He never would have fitted through here," she muttered to herself as she crept upward. The farther she went, the fouler the air became, and at times she had to fight to prevent herself from gagging. She wondered for a moment about how she would convince Giles to commit himself to the reeking confines of the tunnel. She recalled Will's comment with a savage grin. Maybe I'll have to knock him out and shove him down ahead of me, she thought.

She had been crawling uphill for some minutes when she heard a noise echoing from far above her. It was the sound of metal striking and scraping against rock, followed by a low rumbling sound that was gradually growing louder. She paused for a few seconds, puzzling over what was causing it.

Then realization hit her. Someone had just emptied a load of garbage into the chute and it was now tumbling down toward her. A second later, she heard a rush of water as a bucket or barrel was emptied into the chute to flush the new load of garbage out.

She just had time to raise the lantern hard against the roof of the tunnel. Once it was flooding downhill, the water would be confined to the lower half of the tunnel, she reasoned. Then she was deluged with water and a barrage of kitchen waste tumbling down from above.

Her body formed an effective barrier and most of the detritus gathered around her shoulders and head, unable to get past. Much of the water stayed there as well and she finally managed to push herself up on her elbows and knees and allow the water to wash most of the rubbish through with it. She prayed that there was only one load to be dumped as she spluttered and gasped, shaking herself to free the remaining items that were still piled above her.

Fortunately, her quick decision to hold the lantern against the roof had been effective and the tiny yellow light inside it still gleamed, reflecting off the wet rock above and around her. Relighting the lantern in this cramped and airless space would have been extremely difficult, if not impossible, she realized.

She waited for thirty seconds, but it seemed there was no more garbage to be disposed of. Shaking herself again to dislodge a few remaining items, she resumed her painstaking crawl up the tunnel, the flickering flame of the lantern showing her the way once more.

The moisture on her face made her aware of a faint current of air flowing down from above—fresh, clean air, not the stench-ridden atmosphere she had become accustomed to. She realized she must be reaching the end of the climb. She set the lantern down on the floor of the tunnel and inched forward, so that its light was behind her. Without the small flame to dazzle her vision, she could see a faint circle above her. Not light, she realized, but a diminution of the darkness of the tunnel.

She retrieved the lantern and moved on, holding it behind her so that it wouldn't destroy her night vision. Gradually, the small patch of lightness ahead of her grew brighter and larger, and she was conscious that the slope of the tunnel was becoming more acute. She could no longer crawl forward. She had to wedge her shoulders and feet against the walls of the chute and shove herself upward.

After a few minutes, the light ahead was discernible as the mouth of the chute. She increased her pace, setting her shoulders, shoving against the side of the tunnel with her braced feet, then allowing her shoulders to relax so that she moved upward half a meter at a time, then repeating the actions.

Now was the time of greatest danger for her. If someone decided to dump a pail of garbage down the chute now, she would almost certainly be seen. She increased her pace, chafing at the time it was taking her to reach the tunnel mouth. She reasoned that it must be close to midnight by now and the likelihood that anyone would be dumping rubbish was slight. But still her heart pounded and her breath came a little faster.

Then she was at the tunnel mouth, at the top end of the chute. She stopped just below the surface, listening to hear if there was anybody moving close by. She heard nothing, except for the pounding of blood in her ears. After waiting for several seconds, she put her arms out of the tunnel, seized the edges and levered herself up and out in one convulsive movement, dropping to a crouch as she emerged into the kitchen, her hand on the hilt of her saxe.

Massive ovens were ranged along one wall, their fires banked for the night and emitting a dull red glow through the bars of the grates. In the morning, the kitchen staff would open the air vents to increase the draft and add fresh kindling on the banked coals to set the blaze flaring again. For the moment, there was no movement, no sign of anyone in the kitchens. She was aware that in some castles—Redmont, for example—the lower-ranked kitchen staff were allowed to sleep in the kitchens, enjoying the warmth afforded there. But here there was nobody.

Long preparation tables ran down the center of the room,

cleaned and tidied now, with rows of copper pans and pots suspended above them.

She drew her saxe and, holding it ready, took a pace forward. She stopped as something squished under her boot and she glanced down, realizing it was a piece of garbage she had picked up in her long underground journey. She scraped it off against a bench leg, grimacing her distaste as she did.

She could see a flight of stairs—wide stone steps—at the end of the long, dim room and realized she was in the lower kitchen level. She made her way silently toward them and began to climb.

The upper kitchens, where dishes were carved, decorated and prepared for serving, were empty as well.

"Hope nobody calls for a midnight snack," she muttered to herself, and, staying in the shadows close to the wall, ghosted along the room to the large double doors that led to the dining hall.

The tables and benches were empty and half the curtains covering the sleeping niches along the walls were drawn. The others were left open, displaying made-up beds. Judging by the lateness of the hour and the silence throughout the keep, she assumed that these sleeping spots were currently unoccupied. A closer look showed her that there were no personal belongings hanging from the storage hooks there and she realized she was right. She recalled Will's earlier comment about the search parties leaving the chateau short-handed. The regular occupants of most of these beds were probably well away from the castle, on a wild-goose chase for the three escapees.

Occasionally, a sleeper would cough or turn restlessly under the blankets. That was a good sign, she thought. Absolute silence would mean people were awake and listening, that her presence had been discovered. Across the room, someone sneezed violently, muttered, then rolled over in bed.

"Bless you," Maddie said to herself. Then she moved toward the door leading to the anteroom on the ground floor of the keep.

Like the kitchens, the big anteroom was deserted, dimly lit by a series of flambeaus placed in sockets around the walls. She moved though the flickering shadows these torches cast, matching the speed and rhythm of her movements to the flickering, uncertain light and blending in with her surroundings until she was almost completely invisible.

"Hiding in plain sight," Will called it, and it was a skill that all Rangers practiced constantly until it became second nature to them. She reached the big main door leading out into the courtyard. Carefully, she lifted the locking bar out of its iron brackets and set it beside the door. Then she opened the door and slipped out into the courtyard.

29

Keeping close to the wall, Maddie crept along the front of the keep to the corner opposite the southwest tower. During the time when she and Will had been imprisoned, Halt had determined that Giles was back in his former tower room.

But now two guards had been permanently stationed at the point where the battlements met the tower, effectively preventing any attempt to access Giles's upper-floor room by climbing the outside of the tower wall. If Maddie were to attempt it, she would be seen and the alarm would be raised.

This left only one alternative. She would have to enter the tower at ground level and slip past the guardroom that opened onto the battlements. Previous experience had shown them that the stairs were in view of the guardroom and anyone climbing them would be visible to the half dozen guards normally relaxing off duty there. On their previous rescue attempt, they had deemed this too risky.

However, the situation had changed. With over half the garrison out searching for the escaped Rangers, the castle was shorthanded. And with the additional guards assigned on either side of the tower to watch for climbers, this would leave only two or three off duty in the guardroom. And chances were, they would be asleep. The three Rangers had discussed the situation and agreed that Maddie's best course would be to use the internal stairs and trust to her covert movement skills to avoid being seen.

The return journey, with Giles, was another matter. But she would face that when the time came. It would be well after midnight when they descended the stairs, and the guards' watchfulness would be at a low ebb.

She studied the battlements and the movement of the sentries stationed there. They walked their regular patrols and, as ever, their attention was focused outside the castle. The two sentries posted to guard the tower itself had their backs to the courtyard as they kept watch on the curved wall above them. A glance to either side told her there was nobody moving in the courtyard itself. Taking a deep breath, she slipped across the flagstones to the door that led into the tower.

She reached the base of the tower without being seen and flattened herself against the rough stonework beside the door. She could hear the measured tread of the sentries on the battlements above her, as they paced back and forth, their eyes probing the night beyond the chateau's walls for any sign of attack. The fact that they did this night after night, with no sign of impending danger, tended to blunt their vigilance. Night after night, week after week, month after month, they saw nothing untoward. And because they saw nothing time after time, they expected to see nothing. If there had been an enemy making repeated, probing attacks and testing the chateau's defenses, they would have been alert and on their toes. As it was, their senses were dulled and they simply went through the motions.

All of which was in Maddie's favor. Bored guards who were only half alert would tend to discount any slight sounds they might hear or movement they might sense. Nothing ever happened, so they assumed nothing *would* happen.

She heard a faint murmur of lowered voices as two of the guards stopped at the end of their allotted beats and paused to talk. Taking advantage of the fact that their voices would mask any slight sound she might make, she took hold of the iron ring that formed the door handle and twisted it experimentally. The ring turned, lifting the tongue of the latch inside the door. She pushed against the timber and the door gave inward, swinging silently on well-maintained hinges. She made a mental note that such attention to maintenance might seem like good management, but in fact it was a security risk. A noisy, squeaking door opening on rusty hinges would help defenders detect an intruder trying to make their way inside.

She shrugged to herself. That was Lassigny's problem, not hers. She widened the opening a little and slipped inside, closing and latching the door behind her, leaning her back against it while she listened for any sound of movement nearby and let her heart rate settle as her eyes became accustomed to the gloom.

Satisfied that nobody had seen or heard her, she walked silently toward the stairs, which she could now make out in the dim light, curving away up to the higher levels. She tested the first with the toe of her boot. The stairs were wood, which might well mean they were constructed with intentionally squeaky steps. Staying to the sides, where the movement in any loose board would be minimal, she climbed quickly to the next level. She paused again, listening. Hearing nothing, she went up the next flight like a ghost. Once again, there was no sight or sound of anyone so she continued. This next floor would be the tricky one. She was coming to the level of the battlement walkway, and the guards' ready room. She paused with her head just above floor level, her eyes flicking back and forth, her ears seeking the slightest sound of alarm.

Muted sounds of conversation reached her and she listened attentively for a minute or so. Two voices, no more, she thought. She peered between the banister rails and could make out the interior of the guardroom opposite, dimly lit by a single lantern. Two figures were hunched over a bare wooden table in the middle of the room. A one-candle lantern was on the table between them and she realized that, dim though it might be, it would effectively dazzle their eyes and ruin their night vision if they looked away toward the dark outline of the door, and the stairwell beyond it.

She moved on, making no sound as she rounded the banister post and took the next flight up. As soon as she was on the reverse flight, she was effectively out of sight from the guardroom. Heaving a small sigh of relief, she continued upward, pausing at the top of each flight to check for any signs of danger.

The seventh, or penultimate, flight, was where Giles was being held. She paused below the top of the flight this time, all her senses alert, listening. Giles's room was off to her left and she turned her attention this way. For some seconds, she heard nothing and was about to continue moving upward. Then a chair creaked as its occupant shifted his weight, and she heard a voice ask a question. But its owner spoke in Gallic so she didn't understand it.

Dropping to her hands and knees, she crept up until her eyes were just above floor level. Sure enough, there were two armed guards sitting in wooden and canvas chairs outside a door some seven meters away from her.

She went back down a few steps to be out of sight and unwound the sling from her forearm. The men were both wearing felt caps, not helmets, and she nodded in satisfaction as she plucked two stones from her shot bag. The caps would protect them, so that the shot would stun them, not kill them. She fitted a stone to the pouch of her sling and, moving in a crouch, stepped up and out of the stairs onto the seventh floor, letting the weighted sling hang down behind her and holding the second stone ready in her left hand.

She had already decided to target the guard farthest from her. He was half facing in her direction, while his companion had his back to the stairs. She took half a pace forward and whipped the sling up and over, releasing at the final moment as it reached maximum speed.

The smooth, rounded stone slammed into the guard's forehead, just above the rim of his felt cap. He gave a startled grunt, threw out his arms and crashed over, taking the chair with him as he sprawled unconscious on the floor.

As she had expected, the second guard rose hurriedly from his chair and moved to check his stricken companion. That momentary uncertainty gave her the time she needed to reload the sling. As the confused guard turned to face her, she released.

Thud!

The impact of the stone on the man's head—once again above the brim of his felt cap—was sickening. Like his comrade, the guard threw out his arms and collapsed backward onto the floor, half across his partner's still body.

Stowing the sling in a side pocket, Maddie drew her saxe and strode swiftly along the corridor to the two unconscious guards. They were both breathing heavily and she noted that with relief—she had no wish to kill innocent men doing their duty, no matter who they worked for. She knelt beside the second guard and gently rolled back his eyelid. His eye was glazed and unfocused. He was well and truly knocked out and would probably remain so for some time. A quick glance showed her that his companion was in the same condition. She nodded in satisfaction and unhooked a large key ring from the second man's belt. She re-sheathed her saxe and stood, turning her attention to the door as she flicked through the keys on the ring, looking for the most likely one.

It turned out to be the second that she tried. The lock clicked and the door swung open a few centimeters. Putting her shoulder to it, she shoved it open and stepped into the room.

Giles was on the bed, cowering back away from the door, with his knees drawn up.

"What do you want?" he asked in a quavering voice. "Who are you?" Then, as Maddie moved closer, he let out a small squawk of recognition. "You! How did you get here? They said you'd escaped and gone back to Araluen!"

"As you can see, we didn't get far," Maddie told him. She took another pace closer to the bed and he shrank back, pulling the blanket up to his chin in a ridiculous, infantile gesture. Maddie rolled her eyes at him in utter disdain.

"Why don't you pull it up over your head?" she asked sarcastically. "Maybe that'll make me go away."

"What do you want?" he asked again, then, with a shrill note in his voice, he said, "Go away! Leave me alone!"

"Sorry," she said brusquely, "that's not going to happen. We're getting out of here and you're going back to your father."

His eyes widened in fear at her words. "No!" he shrilled. "They'll hurt me if I try to escape again. He said so."

"Again?" Maddie queried. "You didn't actually put in such a great effort last time as I recall. And who said he'll hurt you?"

"The Baron," Giles replied, peering around as if the mere mention of his name might make Lassigny appear, like some evil spirit.

Maddie realized he was paralyzed with fear. To get him moving, she was going to have to put a bigger fear in his mind. She didn't have time to talk to him or reason with him. The longer they delayed, the greater danger they were in. Slowly, she withdrew her saxe. The light of the single candle on the table caught the blade, sending reflections rippling across the wall.

"You spineless little twerp," she said in a hard voice. "Get out of that bed and get your shoes on or I'll separate you from your ears."

That seemed to do the trick. Sniveling miserably, Giles pushed the blanket down and swung his legs over the side of the bed, groping blindly for his shoes with his bare feet. He finally located them and shoved his feet into them.

Maddie sighed in exasperation. "Wrong feet," she told him.

She couldn't afford to have him blundering down the stairs with his shoes on the wrong feet. He was liable to trip and alert the guards below. Hastily, his eyes fixed on the glittering saxe, he switched his feet in the shoes then stood up. As he did, he continued to cringe away from her.

"Get a move on!" she ordered, gesturing with the saxe.

Reluctantly, Giles moved to the door, whimpering quietly.

Lord help this country, Maddie thought, if he ever becomes king. She opened the door and shoved him out. He stopped with a little squawk as he saw the two still figures sprawled on the floor.

"Are they dead?" he asked.

"As doornails," Maddie lied. She figured it was best to make him think she was a ruthless killer. "And so will you be if you don't get moving."

Fearfully, looking back over his shoulder as he went, Giles headed for the stairway, with Maddie close behind. He continued to emit little mewling sounds, and at the top of the stairs, she stopped him, her hand on his shoulder, leaning in close so that his eyes were fixed on her.

"Listen to me," she said. "There are guards down below and if you don't stop whining, they'll hear you. Now stop your noise or I'll finish you and leave you. Your father would prefer to have you back alive. But if you're dead, Lassigny can't use you as a bargaining chip. Understand?"

Of course, she had no intention of killing him and leaving him. But he wasn't to know that. If Maddie were older and more experienced, she might have been able to convince him to trust her with calm, reasoned arguments and reassurance. But she was young and nervous herself, and she was fighting a rising tide of panic as Giles continued to waste time and delay their escape. Furthermore, she sensed that Giles was less inclined to trust her for the simple reason that she was a girl and his background and upbringing worked against it. The only resort that she could see was to instill a sense of fear in him.

He saw the grim determination on her face, looked once more at that razor-sharp saxe and nodded emphatically. Maddie shoved him back toward the stairwell.

"Good. Now keep moving and keep quiet," she told him, and started him down the stairs.

30

ALL WENT WELL UNTIL THEY REACHED THE LANDING ABOVE the guardroom. As they rounded the curve in the stairwell, Maddie became aware of a low murmur of voices coming from below. She held up a hand to stop Giles, who was following two stairs behind her. Turning toward him, she mouthed the words, *Stay here*, and proceeded down a few more steps.

Her heart sank as she made out two dark shapes on the stairs outside the open guardroom door. Two of the guards had decided to move out onto the stairs, where they were sitting and passing a flask of wine back and forth.

Maddie seethed with impatience. She had no way of knowing how many guards were still inside the guardroom, and whether or not they were awake. If she tried to disable the men sitting on the steps, as she had done with the guards outside Giles's room, there was every chance that someone in the guardroom might see them fall and raise the alarm. She decided she would just have to wait them out—wait for them to grow weary or to finish their wine and go back inside. As she crouched on the steps watching them, she became aware of a low, keening sound coming from where she had left Giles. She could only just hear it, but it was gradually growing in volume and it was only a matter of time before the guards below her noticed it. Hastily, she stole back up the stairs.

Giles was sitting on a step, concealed from the guards below by the curvature of the staircase. He was rocking back and forth, his head in his hands, moaning with fright, and as he rocked, the moaning was becoming progressively louder. She crouched beside him, placing her mouth a few centimeters away from his ear. He continued to rock and moan, unaware of her presence. Mindful that if she acted suddenly he might cry out, she touched his shoulder gently with her hand.

"Giles," she whispered, "it's all right. Settle down."

But the rocking and moaning continued, a little louder again. She glanced around desperately.

"Shut up!" she hissed at him, but he continued as if she weren't there. She decided she was going to have to shock him out of it and risk the noise. She drew back a hand and slapped him hard across the cheek.

Instantly, he sat up, his eyes wide-open, looking around. The moaning stopped and he looked at her, not comprehending what had happened. She leaned in close to him.

"Be quiet," she whispered. "Be quiet or they'll hear you."

He opened his mouth to reply but she instantly clamped her hand across it to silence him. Fearfully, she glanced down the stairs. She couldn't see the guards now but she could hear that they had stopped talking. Obviously, the sharp sound of the slap had been heard. She waited, holding her breath, catching Giles's eyes with hers and shaking her head emphatically to forestall any sound he might make.

Then, one of the men below spoke. The language was Gallican

and she couldn't understand the words he said, but the tone was unmistakable. He was querying the slapping noise they had heard. The other man replied but his tone was more relaxed, even dismissive. He didn't think the noise was significant and he seemed to be urging his friend to ignore it. Eventually the first man grunted in agreement, and Maddie heard a sloshing sound as the near-empty flask of wine was tilted and one of the men took another long swig.

Finish the wine and go to bed! she urged them silently. The desultory conversation resumed. Evidently the first man's suspicions were allayed. But still they remained on the steps, relaxing and talking. Maddie began to grow anxious. How long were they going to stay there? Already, time was slipping away. If they remained where they were for too much longer, the castle staff would begin to wake and go about their daily tasks. And that meant the kitchen would be full of people, preventing her and Giles from escaping back down the rubbish chute. And even if they could manage to get down, they could well find themselves emerging in daylight and in full view of any observer who might be on the battlements.

Giles wriggled in protest and she realized she still had her hand clamped over his mouth. Slowly, she released him, but did so with a warning glare that told him not to make a sound. His eyes were wide with fright and he nodded several times. They sat in silence together, waiting for the two drinkers to make a move.

She guessed that it was at least thirty minutes more before she heard the scuffing of boots on the stairs as they rose, stretched and slowly went back into the guardroom. She looked at Giles and mouthed the words, *Stay here*. Then she rose and moved silently down the steps until she could see that the men were gone. The door into the guardroom was half closed, which should hide her and Giles as they passed by on their way down. She hurried back up the stairs to where Giles waited, and held out her hand to help him to his feet. Then she led the way down, moving slowly to avoid any noise. The two drinkers might still be awake, after all.

But there was no cry of alarm as they passed by the door, slipping by silently in the shadow of the staircase. There was a dim lantern still burning inside the guardroom, which helped conceal them as they went past the door, making the darkened stairwell seem even darker by comparison.

At least now Giles wasn't resisting or protesting. He seemed to have accepted the situation and followed obediently in her footsteps as they covered the last few flights of stairs to ground level.

As she reached the door to the courtyard, she held up her hand, signaling for Giles to stop. Moving to the door, she raised the latch and carefully eased the door open a few centimeters, peering out into the courtyard.

There was nobody in sight and she heaved a sigh of relief. Still, she paused. She knew there was a regular foot patrol in the courtyard during the night. If they appeared from behind the keep while she and Giles were crossing the courtyard, the alarm would be raised. She didn't know their schedule or whether the patrol was continuous. She was tempted to wait a few minutes to see if they passed, but rejected the idea. It was already close to dawn, she realized, and she had to make up the time they had lost on the stairs. Coming to a decision, she stepped back, took a firm grip on Giles's arm and led him out into the open space, closing the door behind them.

For a second or two, Giles resisted as they stepped out into the open. But she glared at him and tugged on his arm, half dragging him across the courtyard to the keep. As they went, she felt horribly vulnerable. Her back crawled as she imagined the guards above catching sight of the two moving figures, leveling crossbows at them and reaching for the alarm bells. Giles resisted her, tugging back against her grip, and she pulled all the more firmly, forcing her unwilling companion to move faster.

They stole along the keep's wall to the main door, and she opened it and ushered Giles through to the inside.

She took a few seconds to replace the locking bar on the door. There was no point leaving it unlocked—that would only cause suspicion and possibly raise the alarm within the chateau. Once the door was fastened, she led the way across the ground floor to the kitchen entrance.

She peered carefully around the door, but the vast room was empty and lit only by a few lanterns set against the walls. The long preparation tables stretched away into the shadowy distance. She heard a door bang somewhere nearby, and hurrying footsteps approaching. There was no time to lose. She dragged the hapless prince, half running, across the room to the stairs that led to the lower kitchen. Giles stumbled as they went but she dragged him upright and kept moving. They reached the stairs and she went down without hesitation, her skin crawling, her nerves stretched to breaking point as she waited for a warning cry from behind.

But there was no outcry, no sign that they had been seen, and she slackened their pace as they continued down the wide stone stairs.

"Last thing I need now is for you to trip and break your

ankle," she said in a low voice. Giles gave vent to another soft whimper in reply.

They reached the mouth of the rubbish chute and she paused, taking out her lantern and her flint and tinder and lighting the lamp once more. She could hear voices and movement coming from the upper kitchen now and she had to force herself not to rush. The little light flared inside the lantern, growing brighter as the reflecting plate magnified and focused the glow of the flame. She pointed to the chute.

"In you go," she said.

For a moment, Giles stared at her, a puzzled expression on his face. Then he realized what she wanted him to do and shook his head violently, recoiling from the dark hole that led down into the disposal chute.

"Get in!" she ordered. The voices from upstairs were clearer now and it was only a matter of time before someone came down to the lower room and discovered them. But Giles refused. He shook his head and whimpered and she could see the whites of his fear-widened eyes.

"Come on, you big ninny!" she urged, but still he refused, edging along the wall away from the chute. Her hand went into her side pocket and closed over the cold brass cylinder of her striker. She set the lantern on the table and withdrew the striker, wrapped in her fist. With her left hand, she pointed toward the ceiling.

"Well, we can't go that way," she said, and as she had hoped, he raised his head to look in the direction she was pointing, exposing his jaw to her as he did.

"Sorry about this," she muttered, and swung her loaded fist in a short, fast right hook to his jaw.

Giles's eyes glazed and his knees sagged under him. She caught him before he could fall and dragged him, dazed and staggering, to the chute. She got an arm under his legs and, with the strength of sheer desperation, lifted him, feet first, into the top of the chute, face upward. She lowered him into the dark hole, taking hold of his hands as he went so that his arms were outstretched above his head. That way, there was less chance that he could spread his arms and stop sliding down, blocking the tunnel for her. She bent over the entrance to the chute, holding him by the wrists as she lowered him farther. Then, when she was at the limit of her reach, she released him, giving him an extra push as she did. She heard him sliding away down the stone tunnel, worn smooth over the years by loads of refuse and the many buckets of water used to flush it away. That thought gave her an idea and she glanced around, her eyes lighting on a large bucket standing close by. It was full of water, standing ready to flush down the next load of garbage to be dumped.

That'll make things slide easier, she thought, and she dragged the heavy bucket to the chute. She used her knees and thigh muscles to raise it to the edge, and tipped it in. The water rushed away and she heard a faint yelp from below. She retrieved her lantern and sat on the edge of the chute for a moment. Then she swung her legs up and into the tunnel and shoved off on her back, holding her arms crossed on her chest.

The smooth rock, lubricated by the water she had just poured in, offered little resistance and she slid down the chute, gathering speed as she went. She had a momentary concern as to what might happen if Giles had managed to stop his own descent, blocking the tunnel. But then she dismissed the thought.

"I guess I'll just get him moving again," she said to herself as the sides of the tunnel rushed past her, dimly seen in the flickering light of her lantern.

She was moving faster on the way down than she had when she crawled painfully up several hours before. Lying on her back as she was, she couldn't look down the tunnel to judge her progress, but she felt the slope decrease as she reached the lower section. She continued to slide, her speed falling away, but she was still moving fast when she suddenly emerged into light at the end of the chute, tumbling painfully over the rocks, squishing through the remnants of the last garbage load and finally raising a grunt of pain from Giles as her feet slammed into his ribs where he lay, still dazed, below the outlet from the tunnel.

She raised her head warily, grunting with pain from several bruises caused by the impact with the rocks. The sun had risen and the light dazzled her eyes after the darkness of the tunnel.

"I guess we made it," she said.

Giles didn't reply.

31

"MADDIE!" SHE HEARD WILL'S URGENT CALL AND ROSE PAIN-fully to her feet, looking across the narrow inlet to where he crouched behind a jumble of rocks. He held the coiled rope in one hand, ready to throw it, and she waved to let him know she was ready.

The rope snaked across the intervening gap and landed among the rocks beside her. She grabbed the end and hurried to where Giles was beginning to stir, coming to his hands and knees and moaning softly.

"That's all you ever do," she muttered, and tied the rope around his chest. He looked up at her, uncomprehending, and she got her hands under his arms and hauled him roughly to his feet. There was no time now to strip off her outer clothing as she had done before. Any moment now, someone on the battlements might spot them and sound the alarm. She urged Giles over the rocks toward the water, glancing to where Will stood ready to haul them across.

"Hurry!" he called, trying to project his voice to her and, at the same time, keep it to a whisper. The result was a hoarse, strangled croak. She waved a hand in acknowledgment.

"I'm going as fast as I can," she said, but she knew he wouldn't hear her. Giles stumbled several times on the rocky slope and she finally took hold of the back of his collar to keep him upright. They reached the water's edge and he stopped, setting his feet and resisting her attempts to make him move.

"Come on!" she hissed at him, but he continued to balk, refusing to go any farther.

"Sometimes I wonder why I'm bothering with you," she said. Then she wrapped her arms around him and leaped into the surging water, taking the reluctant prince with her. Instantly, Will began to haul in the rope. They went under for a few seconds, but the tug of the rope brought them to the surface and she clung desperately to Giles as Will pulled them through the turbulent water to safety. In less than a minute, they were across, and Giles, spluttering and gasping, sprawled at the water's edge. Will hurried to grab him by the collar and heave him up onto the rocks. Maddie followed, rising from the water dripping wet and soaked through. Will handed her her cloak.

"Here. Put this on," he said, and she swung the cloak around her shoulders, wrapping herself in its warmth. Will hesitated, looking at Giles, also sodden.

"I don't have anything for him," he said. Then he reached up to unfasten his own cloak. But Maddie stopped him.

"That's his bad luck," she said callously. "He'll just have to shiver." Suddenly, the thought of Will providing his own cloak to the spoiled, self-centered Gallican prince was too much for her. Giles had shown no gratitude or willingness to cooperate in his own rescue. As far as she was concerned, he could freeze. She jerked a thumb upward toward the road above them. "Let's go," she said.

Will gave her a curious glance—it was unlike Maddie to be so unsympathetic—then nodded. He took hold of Giles's arm and began to pull him up the slope. Maddie followed behind them, shoving the prince from time to time when he hesitated or tried to stop.

They struggled up the rocky slope, picking their way between and over the boulders that barred their way, slipping and stumbling on the loose stones underfoot. It would have been slow going, even without Giles's seemingly willful refusal to do anything to help. He was a dead weight, needing to be urged and cajoled at every step, slowing their progress to a crawl.

They were a little over halfway to the top when they heard a shout from the chateau's walls. Maddie turned and peered across the chasm that separated them. There were men on the battlements pointing at them and shouting. As she watched, one of them ran toward the gatehouse tower to raise the alarm. She saw two men leveling crossbows at them and heard the two clunking sounds they made as they released. One of the bolts skated off a rock a few meters from her. She didn't see where the other one went. Then, as she watched, one of the crossbowmen threw up his arms, dropped his weapon and fell backward out of sight, onto the platform behind the battlements.

"That'll be Halt," Will told her, when she cast a puzzled glance at him. "He and Horace are waiting at the top for us. He'll keep their heads down."

Even as he spoke, Maddie saw another guard on the battlement go down. A bell began to sound the alarm in the gatehouse a few seconds later.

"Come on!" Will urged her. "They'll send out a patrol after us any minute!"

Even Giles seemed to realize the urgency of the situation now as they scrambled up the steep rocky slope toward the road. Looking up, Maddie could see Horace leaning over the edge, peering down at them and beckoning for them to increase their pace. But that was easier said than done. The slope was littered with loose rocks and stones and the faster they tried to move, the more they dislodged the uncertain surface under their feet, often sliding and scrabbling back several meters, losing as much ground as they made.

She heard the deep *thrum* of Halt's bow again and again as he forced the men on the battlements to stay down under cover. Panting with exertion, she continued to shove Giles farther and farther up the steep hill in front of her.

"Come on!" Horace was leaning down, his arm outstretched to help them up the final few meters. He seized hold of Giles's hand and heaved him bodily up and onto the level ground of the road. Then Will scrambled up and Maddie followed, her chest and lungs heaving with the effort. For a moment, she stood, regaining her breath and taking stock of the situation.

Halt was watching the battlements, an arrow nocked to his bowstring. The guards on duty had learned their lesson, however, and nobody dared show his face above the battlements. She could make out shapes through the gaps in the crenellations as men moved from one spot to another.

Horace was wearing full chain-mail armor, his round buckler slung over his back and his long sword in its scabbard at his waist. He handed Maddie her bow and a quiver of arrows. She nodded her thanks and clipped the quiver to her belt. She saw Will was similarly armed. A few meters behind them, Tug and Bumper whinnied a greeting. Abelard and Stamper also stood

ready, with a fifth horse, presumably intended for Giles, teth-
ered close by.

"What kept you?" Horace asked. "We expected you'd be well
clear of the chateau by now."

She grimaced at him and jerked a thumb toward Giles.
"Blame him," she said. "He fought me every inch of the way."

In fact, of course, it had been the presence of the two guards
on the stairs that had caused the biggest delay. But she was feeling too unkindly disposed toward Giles to mention that. Horace
looked at the prince, standing miserably by and dripping water
onto the road. He opened his mouth to say something when a
horn blared from the chateau and interrupted him.

The guard at either side of the gate stood aside as a body of
men rode out onto the drawbridge, then clattered across to the
start of the causeway. There were ten fully armed riders, led by
Lassigny himself. He held up a hand to halt the men behind
him, while he studied the small group at the far side of the
causeway.

"Do we run or fight?" Horace asked, moving toward Stamper.

"Fight," Will replied. "If we try to run for it, Giles will never
stay in the saddle."

Horace looked at the prince, noting his unathletic physique
and the all-too-apparent lack of confidence in his bearing. He
nodded agreement and swung up into the saddle in one smooth
move. The three Rangers fanned out across the narrow road
beside him, bows ready and arrows nocked. Giles instinctively
moved behind them for protection.

From the far side of the causeway, Lassigny watched closely.
He saw one mounted knight and three unarmored bowmen

facing him. Being a Gallican, he had no experience of the power and accuracy of the Araluen war bow. It was a weapon he had never faced. Maddie's bout with Armand hadn't added to his knowledge of or respect for the longbow's capability. As far as he was concerned, her victory had been due to trickery and cunning tactics, and her arrows had never actually pierced Armand's defenses. In Lassigny's view, a bow was a hunting weapon, dangerous against animals and perhaps unarmed men.

It held little fear for an armored knight like himself and the ten men with him. He raised his lance and brandished it above his head.

"Charge!" he ordered, setting the lance as he drove his spurs into his battlehorse.

Horace waited impassively. Beneath him, Stamper shifted his feet and shook his mane, reacting to the sight of the approaching horsemen. Horace calmed him, touching him lightly on the neck. He turned to the three Rangers, ready now beside him.

"We want Lassigny alive," he said.

Halt nodded, then spoke to his two companions. "As we face them," he said. Will and Maddie understood the command. It meant they were each to engage the horseman directly facing them, avoiding having two of them aim at the same target. "Ready," Halt continued.

They raised their bows and drew back.

"Release," Halt said calmly, and three arrows streaked away toward the charging men-at-arms.

32

The result was devastating.

The three riders in the front rank behind Lassigny were plucked from their saddles. Two of them lay where they fell. The third tried desperately to crawl clear of the galloping horsemen behind him.

The effect on the following rank was equally disastrous. The horses plunged and reared, trying to avoid the fallen men and rearing horses in front of them. One of them swerved too far and lost its footing in the loose rocks at the edge of the causeway, plunging down the steep, scree-littered slope and throwing its rider, who landed badly and lay groaning. Miraculously, the horse managed to retain its footing and scrabbled its way back up to the road, where it galloped off in panic toward the village, its tail high and its head tossing.

Lassigny heard the sound of crashing horses and falling bodies behind him and reined in, as did his followers, who were struggling to maintain control of their confused and frightened mounts. In a matter of seconds, their disciplined charge had been totally disrupted, and almost half their number had been taken out of the combat.

And the three imperturbable cloaked figures remained unmoved and unmoving, each with another arrow nocked, ready to shoot again. One more volley like the first, Lassigny's men realized, and their force would be all but wiped out. The Baron realized it too. He turned his horse to look back, taking in the bodies sprawled on the road, the riderless horses milling aimlessly about and his remaining men refusing to advance farther. The anger rose in him and he shouted abuse at them.

"Cowards!" he roared. "Will you let three men on foot defeat you?"

Unfortunately, it appeared that they most definitely would. None of them made any move to go forward and, in fact, two men in the rear rank had begun to back their horses away. As Lassigny's eye fell on them, they stopped. But it was only too clear that they had lost all stomach for this fight. He knew he had to act quickly—quickly and decisively—before he lost control of them completely. He spun his horse once more and faced the tall knight in the black-and-red surcoat. The blazon on his shield was unfamiliar—a black bear. Obviously, he was a minor Teutlandic knight. The Baron had never seen that particular insignia before so the man had no known reputation as a warrior. Lassigny raised his lance and jabbed it in the knight's direction.

"You!" he shouted. "Let you and me settle this man to man. Fight me! Don't skulk behind those treacherous killers! Face me in fair combat! Let's settle this between us!" As he finished his challenge, he turned back to the men behind him, who were watching impassively. "I'll show you, you cowards!" he shouted at them. "I'll do your job for you!"

He swung his horse again to face the enemy. The knight had

moved his horse forward a few paces and was tugging at a linen cover on his shield—a cover that bore the bear device. As Lassigny watched, he removed the cover and displayed the permanent insignia it had concealed—a green oakleaf.

Lassigny's blood ran cold as he recognized it. The oakleaf knight was a legend in Gallica. He had been renowned, and respected, for a score of years. Renowned and respected—and feared by those who had faced him in combat.

"Wait . . . ," the Baron cried uncertainly. "Who are you? What is your name?"

The tall warrior urged his horse forward a few more steps and drew his sword with a metallic *shriinng*.

"I am Sir Horace of Redmont," he said in a carrying tone. "I'm the Oakleaf Knight of Araluen."

"Wait!" Lassigny called again, his worst fears realized. "This is a mistake! I didn't realize . . ." He hesitated. Behind him, he heard a low murmur of scorn from his men as he tried to back out of the combat that he had offered. Abruptly, he fell silent. If he backed down now, he would lose control of these men. He would possibly lose control of the entire garrison when word got around. His authority rested very much on his reputation and skill as a warrior. He ruled by fear, not by affection. He had no alternative, he realized. He would have to go through with the challenge he had issued. His mouth was dry and he swallowed several times, assessing his opponent more closely.

The Oakleaf Knight was tall and broad shouldered and he sat his horse with an easy, athletic grace. The long sword glittered in the early morning light and he held it casually, point down. The blade had a blueish tinge to it and a wavy pattern ran down its length as it caught the light. The shield, which now revealed the oakleaf design, was a simple round buckler, not the normal kite-shaped shield adopted by most knights. As such, it would protect less of the man's body and legs than a longer shield might. His helmet was a conical cap without a visor, a nasal or cheek plates. All in all, the man's equipment was simple—to the point of being basic. Most importantly, he carried no lance. The long sword was his only major weapon and it would only be dangerous if he got within reach of Lassigny.

Lassigny, on the other hand, had a long kite shield that reached down to his knees, a four-meter lance and a helmet with a full-face visor.

As he made his assessment, the Baron felt his confidence returning. He could beat this man, he realized. Legends, after all, were often overrated, and the Oakleaf Knight had been younger and undoubtedly stronger when he made his reputation. With a growing feeling of confidence, Lassigny used the edge of his shield to slap his visor closed, couched his lance under his arm and urged his battlehorse forward in a charge, its speed gradually increasing as it thundered across the hard-packed surface of the causeway.

Horace rode to meet him, Stamper moving to a canter, then a gallop, his hooves throwing clods of clay and dirt into the air behind him. Horace moved easily in time to the horse's rhythm, his shield across his body and his sword resting comfortably on his shoulder.

The two horses were at full gallop now, thundering toward each other, ears flattened back on their heads. Lassigny lowered his lance point until it was pointing at Horace's feet. Mindful of Maddie's tactic against Armand, he was prepared for Horace to try to deflect his lance high overhead. The lowered lance point would nullify that move, and he would only bring it up to aim at Horace's body at the last minute.

In fact, Horace had the exact opposite intention. As the two horses strained toward each other, he brought his sword off his shoulder, and as Lassigny's lance began to rise, he slammed it down on the point of the weapon, just as the Baron attempted to make his killing thrust.

Lassigny, prepared to resist an upward flick, was caught unprepared for the powerful downward force of Horace's stroke. The point of his lance was hammered violently down, so that it slammed into the ground with the full impetus of his charging battlehorse behind it.

The point caught in the ground before Lassigny could wrench it loose. The shaft of his lance bent alarmingly as the horse continued onward, and the lance point was trapped in the hard ground. Lassigny found himself propelled out of his saddle while his horse galloped away from beneath him. He had the presence of mind to kick his feet out of the stirrups, then he was sailing upward and backward.

For a few seconds, he seemed weightless. Then the lance shaft could bend no farther and it shivered into splinters and he fell, crashing down on his back on the hard-packed ground of the causeway. A cry of agony escaped him as the breath was forced from his lungs. For a second or two, he lay helpless, stranded on his back, his arms and legs scrabbling weakly. Dimly, some ten meters away, he registered that Horace had reined in his horse and was slipping down from the saddle.

But Lassigny was a seasoned warrior. He was winded by the fall but no bones were broken and he had no major injury. He rolled onto his front and rose groggily to his hands and knees, then, using his shield for support, he raised himself to his feet, his chest heaving as he dragged in lungfuls of air.

Horace stood by, waiting for him, his sword and shield ready.

Drawing in deep, shuddering breaths, Lassigny regained his wind and slowly drew his own sword. The two men advanced on each other. When only a few meters separated them, Horace stopped, sword and shield ready, and waited for Lassigny to make the first move. It was his standard tactic, to allow an opponent to wear themselves out with a series of futile, energy-sapping attacks.

Lassigny began to circle, and Horace pivoted slowly to remain facing him. Then the Baron took a long pace forward and brought his sword over in a glittering arc, cutting down at Horace's head and shoulders.

Without any apparent haste, Horace blocked the stroke with his own sword. There was a shrieking clang of metal on metal and the shock of contact flew up Lassigny's arm. Horace's sword didn't waver or give a centimeter. It stopped the stroke the way a rock stops a wave, shattering its force.

Lassigny stepped back a pace, his sword arm throbbing from the contact. Then he moved in again and delivered a rapid flurry of blows—overhead, side strokes, diagonal blows, forehands and backhands. They followed one another with bewildering speed, but each one was firmly blocked or deflected by the gleaming blade in Horace's hand. No matter where Lassigny aimed, that blue-tinged blade was always there to meet his, seemingly without haste, forming a defense that was totally impenetrable.

Lassigny stopped, his chest heaving with the exertion, his arm aching from the repeated impacts with that unmovable blade. He glanced down and noted the half dozen notches in his blade. His opponent's sword was obviously shaped from incredibly hard steel. He stepped back half a pace and studied his opponent. Horace was breathing evenly, standing balanced on the balls of his feet and with his sword and shield ready to provide more of that implacable defense.

The Baron felt a cold hand of fear clutching his heart. He was a highly skilled warrior, who had triumphed in a score of single combats. But Horace was a champion, and the gap between them was insurmountable.

Then Horace attacked.

His sword flashed like blue lightning as he delivered stroke after stroke at Lassigny, one blending into the other in a rapid series of blows that rained down on the Baron from every angle. Lassigny managed to get his sword into place for the first stroke and was devastated by the shattering force behind it. Never had he felt such power and speed. His arm was numbed by the impact and his knees buckled beneath him, forcing him to give ground. He took the next blow on his shield and felt Horace's sword smash through the wood and leather, hacking a huge chunk out of it. Then it was his sword again, and this time he only just managed to get it in place to parry the stroke. He gave ground, retreating across the hard-packed earth, and Horace followed him inexorably, slamming blow after blow against his sword and shield, never pausing for breath.

A wide, sweeping horizontal stroke glanced off Lassigny's blade and smashed into the top of his helmet, snapping the leather chinstrap and sending the helmet flying.

The six men-at-arms rose in their stirrups as one, watching horrified as the helmet rolled and bounced cross the causeway. For a second or so, it seemed that Horace had beheaded his opponent. Then Lassigny shook his head and staggered back another two paces. He had no thought of attacking now. His only goal was survival—and that was looking more and more doubtful with each passing second.

Horace struck again and Lassigny's already-battered shield split in two, the two halves falling from his grip. Feebly, he tried to parry Horace's next stroke, but his sword was smashed out of the way. Then another crushing blow tore it from his grasp and sent it spinning. Lassigny, unarmed and defenseless, dropped to his knees and held out his hands in supplication.

"Yield!" he shouted hoarsely. "I yield! Mercy, for god's sake."

Horace leveled his sword point at Lassigny's throat and looked into his eyes. The man was finished, he saw. Thoroughly demoralized, physically battered and utterly defeated. There was no fight left in him. He had cast the dice and lost.

Horace turned away from him and faced the six men-at-arms who still sat their horses in the middle of the causeway.

"Do any of you want to continue this challenge?" he demanded coldly. The six men refused to meet his gaze. They turned their faces away, shifting awkwardly in their saddles. They knew that Lassigny was a skilled and dangerous fighter— the most capable warrior in Chateau des Falaises. Yet this tall knight had treated him with contempt and swiftly battered him into submission, after withstanding everything that Lassigny could throw against him.

Horace waited a few seconds, saw that they were all cowed, and continued.

"Then I'd advise you to return to the chateau and wait for a new commander. We'll be taking—"

His back was turned and he never saw Lassigny rise unsteadily to his feet, his hand drawing the broad-bladed, heavy dagger from his belt. His face was a mask of hatred as he stepped toward Horace's unprotected back, raising the dagger for a treacherous killing stroke.

The three Rangers shot within the same heartbeat. Three arrows thudded into Lassigny, the force of the triple impact hurling him sideways.

The dagger fell from his hand, ringing on the stones, and he crashed to the ground, lifeless.

33

HORACE TURNED TO REGARD THE STILL FIGURE BEHIND HIM with distaste. He nodded his thanks to the three Rangers, standing ready once more with arrows nocked to their bow-strings. Then he turned back to the mounted men and continued as if nothing had happened to interrupt him.

"I was going to say, we'll be taking him back to La Lumiere for trial. But I suppose that won't be necessary now. Two of you put his body across his horse's back. Then take him back into the castle."

He watched as two of the men slid to the ground and lifted the Baron's body, laying it across the saddle of his horse, then remounted. "I'll speak to the Baroness and the seneschal about what's going to happen here. The King will be appointing a new baron to this chateau. You can either stay on and look for employment with him or leave. It's your choice. Now get going."

Glancing nervously at the three silent Rangers, the troopers wheeled their horses and, leading Lassigny's battlehorse, clattered across the drawbridge into the chateau. The gate guards watched them in wide-eyed wonder as they bore the Baron's body past them. Then Horace turned back to address his three companions.

"Wait here for me. I won't be long."

Maddie took a pace toward him, her face showing the worry she felt. "You're going in there?" she asked incredulously.

Horace smiled reassuringly at her. "I'll be safe. There's no one there who'll want to take up the fight on Lassigny's behalf. I'm sure he wasn't a popular leader."

Will put his hand on Maddie's arm. "Your father's right," he told her. "A snake can't hurt you once its head has been cut off."

"All the same," Halt said as he mounted Abelard, "I'm going with you, Horace. Never hurts to have someone to watch your back."

"If it'll make you feel better," Horace said easily.

Maddie looked gratefully at Halt. "It'll make *me* feel better," she said, and Halt nodded acknowledgment, riding to join Horace as the tall knight urged Stamper across the causeway toward the chateau.

Will and Maddie watched them go. Then Will led her to the roadside, where he sat down on a large boulder. "May as well be comfortable," he said.

Maddie reluctantly joined him, looking back at Giles, who appeared stunned by the turn of events. "What about him?" she asked.

Will threw a glance in the prince's direction. "I don't think he's going anywhere," he said. "And I don't particularly care if he does."

Horace and Halt rode together through the gatehouse. Nobody attempted to stop them. Nobody challenged their presence. They were met with an almost awestruck disbelief by the garrison. Lassigny had been an overbearing figure for years, feared rather than respected by his men. Now he was gone, in a matter of minutes, and the man who had defeated him so quickly and easily was riding into the chateau. It was taking them some time to adjust to this new situation. In fact, none of them really knew what the new situation might be. They half expected Horace to assume control of the castle and its garrison. That was the way things had worked here at Chateau des Falaises for as long as any of them could remember. To the strong went the rewards. Those who had witnessed the combat were fully aware of Horace's overwhelming skill and strength, and they had quickly disseminated the information to their companions.

There was no leader capable of offering a challenge to Horace, and none of the rank and file were willing to. So it was assumed that he would simply take Lassigny's place.

Word had flashed around the chateau about the fall of their baron. As a result, the seneschal, Sir Gaston, was waiting for them in the courtyard, outside the entrance to the keep. He frowned as the two riders approached him. He didn't recognize the taller of the two, but it was obvious that he was the one in charge.

Horace reined in, looking down at the seneschal. To his credit, Sir Gaston showed no sign of fear, but there was an air of caution about him.

"You're the seneschal?" Horace asked. The large bunch of keys at his belt indicated Gaston's position.

He nodded. "Sir Gaston," he said. "And you are?"

"Sir Horace of Redmont, the Oakleaf Knight of Araluen," Horace replied. He had been knighted as a member of Redmont

Battleschool so he preferred that title, even though he was now resident at Castle Araluen and was overall commander of the Araluen army.

"Will you be taking over here?" Gaston asked. He wasn't unduly concerned. He was a skilled manager and as such was a valuable member of the castle staff. He knew his own worth and it was unlikely that he would be dispossessed by a new commander.

But Horace shook his head. "That appointment will be made by your King," he replied. He looked around. There were a dozen or so people in the courtyard, all watching him, with a mixture of expressions—curiosity, wariness and fear prominent among them. "I need to speak with the Baroness. Has she been told of her husband's death?"

Gaston nodded. "She has. She's in her rooms now. Will you come inside to meet with her?"

Horace shook his head. "No. Send someone to bring her down here."

Gaston turned, searching the small crowd watching them, and beckoned to a castle servant. He gave the man orders to inform the Baroness that Horace was waiting to see her in the courtyard, and sent him hurrying into the keep.

Horace waited patiently. He was sure that the Baroness wouldn't treat his summons with any urgency and he was prepared to wait. Stamper flicked his tail at the occasional fly and shifted his feet from time to time. Gaston waited with him, his eyes on the main door to the keep, where the Baroness would appear.

It took just over ten minutes, then the door opened and Baroness Lassigny appeared. Without any sign of haste, she walked down the steps and across the cobblestones to where Horace was waiting. Gaston stepped forward to make introductions but Horace held up a hand to forestall him. The woman was dark-haired, elegant and very beautiful, he saw, and she was expensively dressed in a long blue velvet gown. Her manner was cool and condescending as she waited for him to speak first. Horace said nothing. He wasn't about to play her little game of one-upmanship. They remained looking at each other in silence for almost half a minute. Finally, she felt compelled to break the silence.

"You wanted to speak to me?" she asked haughtily.

"I sent for you," Horace replied, letting her know who was in control of this meeting.

"And who are you?" she asked.

"I'm Sir Horace of Redmont, also known as the Oakleaf Knight," he replied evenly. "I assume that you are the Lady Lassigny, Baroness of this chateau?"

She nodded, saying nothing.

"You've been told that your husband is dead?"

She lifted one eyebrow and nodded. Horace continued. "You have my condolences for your loss," he said.

"Yet you killed him," she said. It wasn't an accusation, simply a statement of fact, pointing out the inconsistency between his expression of condolence and the fact that he was responsible for her husband's death.

He shrugged. "It was his choice. He challenged me."

"Unwisely, it would appear," she said coolly.

Horace raised an eyebrow in his turn. It seemed there was little love lost between the woman and her dead husband. He decided it was time to get down to the matter at hand.

"Your time here is over," he said bluntly. "The King will appoint a new custodian to this chateau. It would probably be best for you if you weren't here when he arrives."

"Or I could remain here as chatelaine," she said.

But he shook his head. "The King will not allow that."

She formed her lips into a moue. "It may not be entirely up to the King," she said. "These castle walls are strong."

He regarded her with a faint smile of admiration. She was a strong and probably resourceful woman.

"Your garrison is weakened," he pointed out. "Do you think those remaining are loyal to you? Will they follow you?"

She paused, looking around the courtyard and surveying the faces of those who were watching this exchange. Then she uttered a reluctant sigh.

"Probably not," she admitted.

She was a realist, Horace thought, and she might not be safe here if there were men among the garrison who harbored ill will toward her or her husband.

"Then it might be safer for you to leave," he said. "I'll give you time to arrange for your husband's funeral."

She shrugged. "Gaston can take care of that."

No love lost there indeed, he thought. But he said nothing for a few seconds. Then he continued. "Do you have somewhere to go, and will you need an escort?"

She shook her head. "My father's lands are in the north and I have my personal guard—four men-at-arms. They'll protect me on the road."

"Very well," he said, relieved to hear that he didn't have to provide an escort for her. He was anxious to be rid of this country and its intrigues. "I suggest you leave as soon as possible. I'll be escorting Prince Giles back to his father, and the King might decide that some punishment is due to anyone who was close to the Baron."

"I'll leave in the morning," she said. Then she regarded him curiously. "You don't plan to take control here yourself?" she asked. "After all, you defeated Lassigny. Most of his men would serve you. You could be an important figure in Gallica."

"I'm not interested," he said simply, and she shrugged.

"That's the way things are done here. Those who are strong enough take what they want."

But Horace shook his head. "That's why I'm not interested," he replied.

34

They stocked up on provisions in Falaise village and left just before noon. They took the mountain road—Will wanted to recover their cart and they agreed that it was unlikely that the washed-out bridge over the River Cygnes, which led to the main road back to the King's chateau, would have been repaired. The bridge was within the territory governed from Chateau des Falaises, and Lassigny struck them as someone without a lot of regard for his civil obligations.

By sunset, they were still several hours away from the village of Entente, where Maddie and Will had performed en route to Falaise. They found a suitable campsite and settled for the night. Will offered to do the cooking and the others pitched in gathering firewood, fetching water from a nearby stream, building a fireplace and setting up the camp.

All except Giles, who sat a little apart from them, watching them work and waiting to be served his evening meal. Maddie caught Will's eye and raised an eyebrow at this spoiled behavior. He shrugged. When it came time to clear and wash their platters, Giles again took no part. But he was happy to accept a cup of coffee—although he sniffed disdainfully as the three Rangers and Horace all eagerly spooned honey into their mugs.

Halt took over the cooking the following morning. After a quick word from Horace, he prepared the meal—bacon and fried potatoes served with slices from a long, light crusty loaf they had bought in Falaise. Giles again waited to be served his meal, and protested indignantly when Halt served up plates to the other three but not him. Maddie grinned to herself as the arrogant prince, face flushed with anger, challenged Halt.

"Where is my breakfast?" he demanded. "I am hungry."

Halt gestured to the fireplace and the skillet he had used. "Bacon and bread are in the pack there. If you're hungry, you'd better cook some for yourself."

Giles bristled indignantly. "I am a prince!" he stated. "I do not cook!"

"Then you do not eat," Horace told him, as he poured himself a cup of coffee.

"But . . . I am of noble birth! I will not demean myself by doing a churl's work!" Giles spluttered.

"Look, Your Highness," Horace said, leaning back against a log set by the fire and sipping his coffee, "we're travelers. We're camping out. Everyone takes their turn doing the 'churl's work,' as you call it. If you don't, you don't get fed."

Giles looked around at the other three, who were all watching with interest—but notably without sympathy. "I shall tell my father—the King," he said, adding the last two words as if this were the crowning argument.

Horace made a small gesture with his right hand. "Go ahead and tell him," he said. "But if you want to threaten us with his royal displeasure, we might just leave you to your own devices and head directly back to Araluen. And you can go on alone."

Giles, thoroughly confused now, looked at the others for some sign of understanding. He found none. In fact, Maddie even added to Horace's threat.

"I doubt you'd survive too long on the road by yourself," she said.

Giles recoiled slightly, realizing that what she said was true. He hesitated for some seconds, then walked uncertainly to the fireplace and began preparing his own breakfast.

Unskilled as he was, he managed to burn the bacon and undercook the potatoes. But he was hungry and wolfed the food down. At least there was little he could do to ruin the bread.

When Giles was finished eating, Horace poured him a cup of coffee. The prince looked up at him in surprise when he offered this. But the tall knight merely indicated that he was welcome to the hot drink.

"This is the way we do it," he told Giles. "We share the work and we share the food. We don't have servants with us. Now, when you've had your coffee, you can clean the platters and cooking utensils while the rest of us break camp."

And so Giles reluctantly learned that, while he might be a pampered prince at Chateau La Lumiere, on the road he was just another traveler. He also learned, somewhat to his surprise, that doing a little hard work might get his hands dirty, but it wasn't fatal.

They recovered the cart from the spot where they had concealed it. Will and Maddie stripped it of its gaudy decorations and banners and they rode on, passing through the village of Entente in the midafternoon.

Michel, the innkeeper, was sitting outside his inn when they rode by. He rose and moved to the edge of the road, flagging down the cart, which Will was driving.

"Good afternoon," he called. "I nearly didn't recognize you."

Will, of course, was dressed now in his plain Ranger's clothing, not the gaudy trappings of a jongleur. He waved a hand in recognition. Michel noticed Maddie, riding a few meters behind the cart, and he sketched a bow in her direction. "Greetings, mistress. Are you planning on gracing us with a performance?"

Maddie smiled. "I don't do that anymore," she said. "It got me into too much trouble last time." When they had passed through Entente on the way to Chateau des Falaises, they had been robbed by a gang of outlaws called the Black Vultures.

"You got your money back, I believe?" Will said, and the innkeeper nodded enthusiastically.

"Yes indeed! It was returned to us by a mysterious archer." He paused, frowning slightly. "He was wearing a cloak rather like the one you've got on. And he rode a horse that looked a lot like that one." He indicated Tug, who was currently harnessed between the shafts of the cart.

"Really?" said Will, maintaining a straight face. "There aren't a lot of them around."

"Do you need rooms for the night?" Michel asked. He had done a quick calculation of the rooms he had available and ascertained that he could fit the party of five in. His guests usually came in ones or twos. Five extra, with five dinners and breakfasts, would turn a tidy profit for him—and an unexpected one. But his face fell when Will glanced at the sun and shook his head.

"Thanks. But we'll push on. We want to reach La Lumiere as soon as possible."

Michel raise a hand in farewell. "More's the pity," he said. Then he added, also maintaining a straight face, "If you run into that archer, give him our thanks."

Will smiled. "We'll do that. Stay well, Michel."

"Travel safely," Michel replied, and stood watching as the little cavalcade trotted off down the main road of the village, earning curious glances from several of the villagers who were out and about.

As he gradually shouldered his share of the work around their little camp, Giles began to unbend and lose some of the starchiness and pomposity that he had displayed on the first day. He found he enjoyed the easy, informal camaraderie around the camp fire each evening, where his fellow travelers joshed one another and joked among themselves. Once they realized he was prepared to share the hard work, they included him in their conversations. They didn't show him any undue deference. Nor, on the other hand, did they show any spite toward him. Even Maddie, who still remembered his infuriating behavior when they were escaping from the chateau, seemed to hold no grudge against him.

One puzzle remained for the Araluens, and Will raised it one evening as they sat around the camp fire.

"I still wonder who betrayed us," he said. He had told Halt and Horace about Lassigny's assertion that a member of Philippe's party in Araluen had betrayed their presence and intentions to the Baron.

Halt raised the time-honored question used to determine guilt. "Who stood to benefit?" he asked. He paused, then added, "Probably none of them, except perhaps Prince Louis."

Maddie frowned at him. "Why would he benefit?"

"If Giles was out of the way, Louis would be the next in line for the throne," Will said. "And after all, he did send a man to spy on us on the road."

Giles had been dozing by the fire, his head nodding, eyes closed. It had been a long day in the saddle and he was only half listening to the discussion. But he registered his uncle's name. He yawned and looked up.

"He came to Chateau des Falaises," he said.

The others fell silent, watching him. Finally, Will asked the question that was on all their lips.

"Who did? Prince Louis? Your uncle?"

Giles nodded, still drowsy and not realizing the importance of what he was saying. "It was shortly after you arrived. I assumed he came to negotiate my release."

"You saw him? You spoke to him?" Halt asked.

Giles shook his head. "A small group of riders came late one night. I heard the horses in the bailey and looked out my window. I thought I recognized the leader but I couldn't be sure." He looked up, half smiling in apology. "It was dark and I couldn't see him clearly. But there was something familiar about him." He yawned again, failing to notice the intense interest of his listeners. "Then, the next morning, while I was being allowed to get some fresh air in the bailey, I passed by a room where someone was singing that song he loves . . ." He paused, trying to remember the song's name.

"'La lune, elle est mon amour'?" Maddie asked slowly.

He smiled at her. "That's the one. Silly nonsense, really. How can the moon be anyone's lover? It's just a thing, after all."

35

They reached Chateau La Lumiere two days later.

There was no large welcoming party waiting for them—they had sent no advance warning and the cart, without all its adornments and banners, didn't merit any undue notice. It wasn't until Giles dismounted, identified himself and began demanding that servants bring him refreshments and treat him with the ceremony and deference due to his rank, that people began to bustle around them and word was sent to the King that his son had returned.

Maddie watched the prince strutting about the castle courtyard and shrugged wearily.

"Didn't take him long to revert to type," she said.

Will grinned wearily at her. "With that type, it never does."

It was noticeable that the King didn't deem it necessary to rush down to the courtyard and welcome his son home. Rather, he sent a courtier to summon Giles to the throne room. Giles departed, without a backward glance at his erstwhile traveling companions, who were left standing uncertainly by the cart. The courtier seemed to realize their absence after a minute or two and hurriedly returned.

"Perhaps you'd better come too," he said, and the four Araluens trooped off after him into the keep.

The double doors providing entry to the throne room were guarded by two men-at-arms. Their guide gestured for the guards to stand aside and the Araluens marched into the room, coming to a halt in front of the throne, where Giles was already seated on a velvet upholstered stool. The throne room was vast and ornately decorated with tapestries and paintings. A huge stained-glass window let in the sun on the southern side, throwing multicolored beams and patterns on the polished wood floor.

Philippe's throne was at one end of the room, on a raised platform. Apart from a line of spindly-legged hard chairs placed against the opposite wall, the room was unfurnished. Half a dozen men-at-arms stood at attention round the walls, all wearing chain mail and carrying long halberds. Several suits of armor were placed around the room, and the two longer walls were hung with a dozen shields, all bearing ornate coats of arms.

Horace gave a perfunctory bow, inclining just his head. The King, sprawling sideways on the large, gilt-encrusted throne, frowned at the lack of deference but decided to let it pass. Horace was a powerful, confident figure and he tended to dominate the room. In addition, the long sword at his side carried its own unspoken threat. Horace had refused to surrender it when he had entered the throne room.

"I don't know you," King Philippe said. His voice was high and rather nasal, Horace noted.

"I am Sir Horace of Redmont, Knight of the Oakleaf," he replied. He was getting a little bored with all this formal stating of titles. "I was present when you met with King Duncan some weeks ago." Obviously, he thought, Philippe didn't take notice of those he presumed to be his inferiors.

"And what are you doing in my country?" Philippe inquired.

"King Duncan sent me, in case his original emissaries needed help." He indicated Will and Maddie, standing a few paces behind him, then added meaningfully, "They did."

Giles, who had half turned on his stool to watch Horace, swiveled back to his father. "It was Sir Horace who killed Lassigny, Father," he said.

Philippe's eyebrows rose. "Lassigny is dead?" he asked. The news hadn't reached him. Giles nodded emphatically, smiling as if it were he who had dealt with the treacherous Baron.

"It took him no more than a few minutes," he said smugly, again seeming to assume some form of responsibility for Horace's actions. "And he banished the Baroness back to her father's estates."

Philippe's raised eyebrows lowered into a scowl. "I would have preferred that she be brought before me," he said. "She was party to her husband's treason and my torturers would have made her welcome here."

Horace demurred. "There was no proof that she was party to the treason, sir," he said.

Philippe turned his gaze back to him. "I'm the King," he said. "I don't need proof." At those words, Horace found himself glad that he had allowed the Baroness to escape. Philippe continued. "And as King, I am addressed as 'Your Majesty.'"

Horace regarded him coolly for several seconds, then replied, "Yes, sir."

Philippe's cheeks flushed but he said nothing. Curse these Araluens with their arrogance and stubbornness, he thought. But he realized that any insistence on his part would be met with refusal and that would result in a loss of dignity. He decided to let the matter pass and covered his anger with a show of magnanimity.

"You have our thanks for returning our son to us," he said, including the other three Araluens in his gaze. "You will dine with us tonight so we can express our gratitude more fully."

He beckoned to the courtier who had escorted them from the courtyard. "Arrange rooms for Sir Horace and his party," he said with a dismissive wave of his hand.

The courtier bowed deeply. "Yes, Your Majesty," he said, wondering where he was supposed to accommodate them. No arrangements had been made, as nobody knew they were coming. And he had no idea of their rank or importance, which might help him determine the standard of rooms they were offered. He decided that such details were beneath the King's attention and beckoned to Horace.

"Come this way."

Horace made another short bow to the King. The three Rangers followed suit, then they all turned on their heels and marched out of the throne room. Maddie noted that the courtier took care to back away from the King, and she grinned to herself. Undoubtedly, they had just committed another gross breach of royal protocol.

The dinner that night was a small affair in the King's private dining room. The four Araluens were present, along with the King, his wife, Angelique, Giles, and Prince Louis, the King's brother. As ever in Chateau La Lumiere, a silent group of half a dozen armed guards flanked the room.

What a way to live, Maddie thought, surveying their grim

faces as she took her seat. Her father didn't deem it necessary to have armed guards present when he dined with his family.

The meal itself was excellent, although Maddie found the profusion of sauces a little rich for her liking. Her father set a far plainer table, making sure that food served was fresh and in season, allowing the ingredients to speak for themselves.

Little was said during the meal, but when the servants cleared away the platters and poured more wine for the King and his family, Philippe sat back expansively and addressed Will.

"So, jongleur, Lassigny saw through your disguise, did he?" He seemed to take a certain degree of pleasure in pointing out that Will and Maddie's true mission had been exposed so quickly. Will glanced at his companions and received a brief nod from Halt and Horace. They had discussed this matter earlier in the evening.

"We were betrayed, sir," he said evenly. Glancing sidelong at Prince Louis, he saw the man flinch violently, then bury his nose deep in a goblet of wine.

The King sat back suddenly in his high-backed chair, his languid and superior air dispelled by the unexpected statement. "Betrayed? By whom? How do you know this?"

"We know because Lassigny himself told us, sir. He said a member of your entourage—the men who traveled with you to Araluen—betrayed our identities and our mission."

Philippe sat forward again and half rose from his chair, his face dark with fury. "One of my men?" he raged. "Who was it? Tell me his name and I'll see the traitor hanged!"

Will shook his head slowly. "The Baron didn't say, sir," he told the King. Still surreptitiously watching Louis, he saw the prince lower his goblet, a look of relief on his face. That's not going to last, he thought grimly.

Philippe lowered himself back into the chair. His eyes were narrowed and his anger was all too apparent. "I'll find out. I'll have every one of them flogged until the traitor is discovered! How dare he betray *me*!"

Will and Maddie exchanged a knowing look. Apparently, Philippe was more concerned that he had been betrayed rather than by the fact that their lives had been placed in jeopardy.

"No need for that, sir," he said. "We know who the traitor was."

"Then give me his name!" Philippe shouted. "Tell me who it was and I'll see him on the gallows!"

"We believe it was Prince Louis, sir," Will said.

The effect on Louis was dramatic. He recoiled in his chair, his eyes wide and panic-stricken. His mouth opened and closed, but for a moment no sound came. Eventually, he managed to mumble a denial.

"No . . . no . . . it's a lie . . . I never . . ."

Philippe's rage was now red-hot. He stood suddenly, his heavy chair crashing over backward, and strode quickly to where his brother sat, gasping and shaking his head, mouthing his denials like a stranded fish. If anything were to convince those watching him of his culpability, it was his reaction—panic, fear and, above all, guilt.

Philippe took him by the lapels of his silk doublet and shook him violently. Louis tried to cower away from his brother, his head snapping back and forth.

"How dare you betray me? You traitor! You snake! How dare you? Why would you do such a thing?" the King raged.

Louis plucked ineffectually at his brother's hands, trying to release them.

"If our mission failed and Giles was out of the way, Louis

became the heir to the throne," Will continued. "The last thing Louis wanted was for Giles to be released."

"He had a man follow us to Chateau des Falaises." Maddie took up the narrative now. "He was spying on us and doubtless would have revealed our identity to Lassigny. Except we caught him and sent him packing."

Philippe's eyes flashed to her, then back again to his wretched, sniveling brother. He released his grip on the doublet and thrust him back into his seat as Will continued the accusation.

"And it was Giles himself who told us that Louis had a secret meeting with Lassigny. He arrived at Chateau des Falaises late one night. At the time, Giles thought his uncle was there to negotiate his release."

He was careful not to say that Giles hadn't actually *seen* his uncle at the Chateau. But the implication was clear and Louis confirmed it for them.

"Yes! Yes! That was it!" he gabbled helplessly. "I went to persuade Lassigny to release Giles! That was all! I never . . ." He stopped as he realized he had just incriminated himself.

Philippe stood over him, hatred replacing the fury in his eyes. "Then you admit you were in contact with Lassigny?" he said grimly.

His brother looked desperately at the accusing faces surrounding him, searching for someone, anyone, who might speak up for him. He was met with stony stares.

"It wasn't like that . . . ," he whimpered.

Philippe turned away from him in disgust. He gestured to the leader of the guard detachment. "Take that treacherous cur away!"

36

HORACE BUCKLED THE LAST STRAP ON HIS SADDLEBAGS AND looked around the room, checking to make sure that he hadn't left anything behind.

Not surprisingly, the dinner the night before had ended abruptly, after Prince Louis was dragged, sniveling and weeping, from the room by the guards. King Philippe had left almost immediately after that, without another word to the four Araluens, his face still suffused with anger. Then Queen Angelique had thanked them for their service and bade them good night as well.

"I'm sure my husband will want to speak to you in the morning," she had said, a note of apology in her voice. It seemed to Maddie that the queen was unsurprised by her husband's fit of anger. Probably used to it, she thought.

They had made their way to the large suite of rooms that had been allotted to them. The courtier had obviously assumed that since they had accompanied Prince Giles and were to dine with the King, they deserved superior accommodation.

In the morning, servants brought them breakfast in the suite, but no word came from Philippe. Horace drained the last of his coffee and looked around at his friends.

"Pack up and let's get out of here," he said. "I'm sick and tired of this wretched country."

Maddie was interested in the way her father assumed command of the group and how Halt and Will, both senior officers in her father's service, deferred to him. Horace sent one of the servants who had brought the breakfast trays to have their horses saddled and the cart made ready for departure. Earlier that morning, he had arranged to buy a sturdy little draft pony for the cart. Tug and Bumper had spent enough time pulling it around Gallica, he said.

"Everyone ready?" he asked.

They all nodded in confirmation. In truth, they had little enough to pack. They trooped out of the apartment behind him and followed him down the stairs to the ground floor. Emerging into the morning sunlight, they saw Stamper and his three smaller companions standing ready. The cart was a few meters away with the new horse ready in the traces.

Horace threw his saddlebags up over Stamper's hindquarters and tied them in place. His round buckler was tied to the saddle as well.

"Sir Horace! Wait!" a voice cried out to him across the courtyard. Sir Guillaume, the gate marshal who had admitted Will and Maddie some weeks previously, was hurrying across the bailey from the gatehouse, waving to catch his attention.

Horace, about to place his foot in the stirrup and swing up into the saddle, paused. Holding Stamper's reins in his left hand, he moved to stand by the horse's head to greet the marshal.

"I'm Sir Guillaume, sir," the marshal said, a little out of breath. He held out his hand and Horace shook it perfunctorily. "I was off duty when you arrived last night," the marshal explained.

Horace said nothing. He had a fairly good idea why Guillaume had stopped them.

After an expectant pause, Sir Guillaume asked, "Where are you going, Sir Horace?" He looked around at the rest of the small party, standing by their horses and the cart, obviously ready to depart. "You're not leaving?"

"I am leaving," Horace told him. "We're all leaving. We're going back to Araluen. We've done what we came to do. Prince Giles has been returned safely."

"But the King will want to speak to you . . . ," Guillaume began uncertainly. The tall knight before him was a grim and unsettling figure. Horace made a derisive gesture at the mention of the King's name.

"With all due respect, Sir Guillaume," he began, then qualified the statement. "Actually, with no respect at all, there's nothing the King can say that I'm interested in hearing."

"But he assumed you would stay to witness the execution," Guillaume continued anxiously. He knew Philippe would be furious if the Araluens simply left, and he knew who would bear the brunt of that fury.

"Execution?" Horace repeated. "Who is to be executed?"

Guillaume frowned in puzzlement. "Why, Prince Louis, of course. For treason."

Horace feigned surprise. "Executed? So he's been tried, convicted and sentenced already, has he? Your courts move fast in this country, I must say."

The marshal shifted uneasily, shrugging his shoulders. Surely it was obvious, he thought. "There was no court. No trial. The King has found him guilty. The evidence was all there."

Horace shook his head in disbelief. The evidence against

Louis was all circumstantial. Of course, Horace firmly believed Louis was guilty of betraying his brother, and Will and Maddie for that matter. But in Araluen, he knew, such evidence as there was would hardly be sufficient to bring in a guilty verdict—certainly not if it carried with it a death sentence.

Banishment, possibly, and forfeiture of titles and property. But certainly not a death sentence.

He recalled Philippe's words when they had discussed Baroness Lassigny: *I'm the King. I don't need proof.* And suddenly he was heartily sick and tired of Gallica, with its never-ending web of intrigues, jealousies, pettiness, treachery and cruelty. He swung up into the saddle and called to his companions.

"Mount up," he called. "Let's get out of this wretched country. We're going home."